The Red Jag

The Red Jag
and Other Stories

Ray French

Planet

First published
in Wales in 2000
by Planet

PO Box 44
Aberystwyth
Ceredigion
Cymru/Wales

Cover design: Glyn Rees

Cover photo of author: Antonio Sanchez

Printed by Gwasg Gomer
Llandysul, Ceredigion

Published with the financial support
of the Arts Council of Wales

ISBN: 0 9505188 7 5

To Joanna

"Freedom is what you do with what's been done to you"
Jean-Paul Sartre

Acknowledgements

I am very grateful to John Barnie, without his enthusiasm, encouragement and patience this book would not exist. I am indebted to Jane Rogers for her insights, suggestions and generosity of spirit. Thanks again to my writing group — Catherine, Eva, Gerry, Ian, Jackie, Jocelyne, and Spike — who read several of these stories in progress. My gratitude also to Laurence, for listening. And thank you to everyone at *Planet*.

I found the following books very helpful: Max Arthur, *Northern Ireland Soldiers Talking* (Sedgwick & Jackson, 1987), and Stephen Jarvis, *The Bizarre Leisure Book* (Robson, 1993).

Contents

THE RED JAG

Someone had pinched dad's bike. He was looking for another one in *The Argus*.

"Gents racer, brand new, unwanted gift."

He drew a circle around the advert with a pen.

"Unwanted gift? Alright for some."

I heard the ice cream van, but it was still a few streets away.

"Ring after six."

He looked at his watch.

"It's twenty to. Better get a move on. Do you want to come with me?"

We went out the back way. Mam was standing next to the fence, talking to Mrs Phillips next door. Colin was standing in mam's flowers, he had the cat by the tail.

"Can I come?"

He was always trying to tag along with us. We should have gone out the front door. But I needn't have worried, dad rushed past without even noticing him. I pointed my finger right in Colin's stupid face, to let him know that if he said anything else I'd get him later. He stared at me with his mouth open. The cat scratched him and he started bawling.

Mam looked round and said

"What is it lovely?"

Then

"Get out of there!"

Colin started screaming. As dad was leaning over to bolt the gate behind us, he looked back at them and sighed.

"She's spoiling him, he'll grow up to be a right mummy's boy."

Mummy's boy, that's what I'd call him from now on.

The first phonebox was broken. There was a lady shouting in

the second one.

"I should have listened to Sheila, she warned me about you."

Dad rolled his eyes, looked at me and said, "God help us."

She slapped the window with her hand.

"Oh come off it, Ronnie."

Dad started pacing up and down, banging the rolled up paper against his leg.

"Come on Ronnie, give us all a break."

He must have known who she was talking to. Dad knew nearly everyone in Pill.

I climbed onto the bench opposite the phonebox and stood on the back of the seat. I could see the platform moving on the Transporter Bridge from up there. Some days I went backwards and forwards over it about twenty times. I wasn't going anywhere, I just liked the ride. I loved watching the careful way they loaded the cars and lorries, packing them on so close there was hardly an inch between them. Then I'd stare down at the river flowing under my feet while we crossed to the other side.

The pips were going. Dad put his hand on the door, ready to open it. I jumped off the bench and stood next to him. The lady held the phone with one hand, rummaged for some more money in her purse with the other.

"Excuse me love," dad started pulling the door open — "Have you finished yet?"

She was making a sort of whimpering noise. I went round to the other side and stared in at her. She pretended not to see me. It was ours now, she'd have to get out, she'd never find more money in time. She turned her purse upside down and emptied everything out. I looked round at dad, he was making a face like Steptoe. When I looked back at the lady she was pushing another two bob piece in. How lucky can you get? Then — I couldn't believe it — she started crying into the phone. What a waste of money!

Dad groaned and let go of the door. He kicked the wall.

"Come on, let's go. We'll be here all night."

There wasn't another phone box nearby that worked, so we walked up through town.

"I'll pop into The Prince of Wales and ring from there."

He looked at his watch and smiled.

"I can get that tenner from Gareth, kill two birds with one stone."

I didn't like him going into pubs. When we went to Barry Island with the Phillipses, him and Mr Phillips spent hours in the pub. Mam and Mrs Phillips kept moaning about it and I got stuck with Colin all afternoon. I made him drink seawater.

The pub was down a narrow alley next to the market.

"Wait here. I won't be a minute."

There was a lettuce lying in the gutter, I kicked it and it rolled under a car. It made me think of salad. I hated salad. The worst thing about it was the way the beetroot juice turned everything else on the plate pink.

Dad came out with a packet of crisps.

"It's engaged, I'm just having a word with Gareth. Here, they're cheese and onion. I won't be a minute."

He ruffled my hair and went back inside. Crisps from the pub always tasted better.

A man staggered past singing *Hey Jude*. He couldn't walk straight. He was a terrible singer too, dad was much better. People were always asking dad to do *Delilah*. He did all the actions, made all the faces, everyone said he should be on the telly.

Dad came out again, looking miserable.

"He says there's two other people coming round to look at it already."

That was it, we had no chance. Whoever got there first would snap up a brand new racer straight away. Dad rubbed his chin.

"He didn't even want to give me the address, but I twisted his arm. Let's see if we can beat the others to it — first come first served. How fast can you walk?"

We went past the ABC. *Bullit* was still on — *Starring Steve McQueen. Retained For Third Great Week!* I'd seen the trailers for it on the telly. There was a fantastic car chase along a really hilly road, cars were going so fast that when they got to the top of a hill they took off into the air with the wheels spinning and when they hit the ground, the drivers bounced up and hit their heads on the roof. I couldn't go and see it though, because it was an A. It wasn't fair.

"Dad, why have they spelt *Bullit* like that? Shouldn't there be an e in it, not an i?"

He didn't hear me, he was annoyed.

"Like trying to get blood out of a stone getting money out of Gareth. I'll pay you back in instalments he said. A pound now, and another pound at the game on Sunday morning."

On Sundays dad and Gareth stood on the touchline and shouted funny things at players who made mistakes, and got everyone laughing at them. Only sometimes the players got angry and shouted things back. Once the goalkeeper was arguing with dad when one of the defenders passed the ball back to him and it went straight into the goal.

The road became steeper, I was starting to sweat. We ran across the big roundabout, dad nodded at all the flowers covering it.

"They wouldn't last five minutes in Pill."

I kicked the heads off some red ones, the petals exploded around me.

By now he was striding along really fast, I had to run a few steps every so often to keep up with him.

"Slow down."

He didn't hear.

"Dad, dad, please slow down."

"I can't, we've got to get there before the others. It'll be all downhill on the way back. We'll be home in no time on that racer. You can sit on the crossbar."

He was wiping sweat from his forehead and blowing out his cheeks. When we got to the top of the road, he took out his handkerchief and wiped his face and neck. I leaned against the wall, panting.

"Tired?"

I nodded, he smiled and ruffled my hair.

"It's not much further. Now you can see why I didn't want to bring Colin."

I was ready to go on again.

We crossed over and walked up Fields Park Crescent. The houses were huge. They weren't joined up, they stood apart from each other. Some of them had ivy growing all over them, and little turrets like you'd see on a castle; one had a tennis court in the garden. Dad put on a posh voice.

"Anyone for tennis? Your point old fruit."

Dad was really funny sometimes, but he didn't make me laugh now. I could tell that even though he was poking fun at it, he was a bit nervous.

"Would you like to live up here?"

The way he was looking at me, I knew it was important to answer the right way. It felt so important I couldn't bring myself to say anything in case it was wrong.

He nodded at a lady sitting in a deckchair, eating ice cream.

"They don't know what it's like to have to scrimp and save and watch every penny. Unwanted gift, Christ!"

There was a man ahead washing his car, a red jag. It was the kind of car Steve McQueen would drive. As we drew closer I slowed down to get a better look. It was the most beautiful car I'd ever seen. I wanted one just like it when I grew up. Every day I'd get up early, to wash and polish it till it shone. I wanted to climb into the driver's seat and hold the steering wheel. I wanted to press the horn, rev the engine up so loud that people had to put their hands over their ears.

Just as dad was about to pass by, the man stepped back right into his path without looking. Dad was going too fast to get out of his way in time. He shouted "Beep beep!" and pushed past him, knocking the bucket out of his hand. Water slopped all over the man's shoes.

The man looked furious. He had a big black moustache just like Wilko, our PE teacher; everybody in school was frightened of him. He muttered something to dad. Dad stared back and said, "You don't own the bloody pavement."

Dad walked on but kept slowing down and looking back. I knew if one of them said anything to the other now, there'd be a fight. I was afraid of the man. Eventually dad stopped looking back and speeded up. The man was still staring though. He was shouting something, but dad ignored him, he was too far back now.

"Flash Harry. His sort never looks out for cyclists. Blokes like him think they own the road just because they've got a flashy car."

I didn't like the way he said *flashy car*, as if it was wrong to want a red jag like his. We didn't say anything else till we reached the house.

"This is it. Number 19."

There was a sign next to the door, it said *Belvedere* in swirly writing. Underneath the letter box it said *No Hawkers*.

"What's a Hawker?"

Dad shushed me. When he rang the bell, a couple of dogs started barking, a big loud one and a small yapping one. The man who answered the door didn't smile. He looked like he knew we'd done something wrong, he just couldn't figure out what it was yet.

"I'm sorry, I sold it to another gentleman five minutes ago."

Dad groaned.

"I did warn you some people were already on their way."

When the man closed the door, dad said, "Typical. That's just my luck."

He was always complaining about his luck, but it was his own fault. We would have been there in time if he hadn't got into that row with the man who owned the red jag.

Dad was really quiet. We were miles from home, and we had to walk back. I started to feel nervous when I remembered we had to pass the man who owned the red jag again. As we got nearer to where he lived I looked at dad and I could tell he was getting nervous too.

But when we reached the man's house there was no sign of him. I felt like cheering. The red jag was still there though, shiny and sparkling in the sun. It looked fantastic now he'd finished washing it. The racing bike was nothing compared to a jag. If only we had a car like that, if only we could have jumped into it and driven home. I bet it would go so fast that when we went over a hill it would fly up into the air with its wheels spinning, like the car in *Bullit*.

"Isn't it brilliant? Red's my favourite colour, Man Utd play in red. When I grow up..."

Dad wasn't listening, he was looking at the house where the man lived. I started getting nervous again. What if he saw us, came out and went for dad? I wouldn't be able to stop him. I looked too, but I couldn't see anyone. Then dad started whistling, walked straight up to the jag, and reached inside his pocket. He looked up and down the road, there was no one else around. He took out his penknife, opened it and walked alongside, slowly scratching the jag from the back wheel to the headlamp. I couldn't believe it. I put my hands over my ears to block out the horrible scraping sound it made. He put the penknife back in his pocket and walked on as if nothing had happened.

I stared at the jagged line. It was like a wound in the car's side. He'd ruined it. I pulled away a big flake of red paint that was hanging off and held it in my fingers. It looked like blood.

He shouldn't have done it.

Someone started banging and shouting behind my back. I turned round and there was the man who owned the jag standing in the window, pointing at me. I ran like mad. When I caught up with dad, he winked at me and said, "That'll teach him."

I tugged at his sleeve.

"Dad he saw me! That man saw me standing by his car."

He shrugged my hand off.

"Don't be stupid. You imagined it."

He never listened. I knew the man would be calling the police right now. He saw me standing next to it, he'd think I'd done it. They'd arrest me, not dad. He started waving me on with his hand.

"Come on. Hurry up!"

I couldn't keep up, he was going too fast. I was getting a stitch. Someone was running after us. They were getting closer.

I hated him.

THE MOST WESTERLY POINT IN EUROPE

Nothing else they'd seen in Kerry had prepared Denis and Julia for the Slea Head road, a narrow ledge blasted out of the cliff face, hundreds of feet above the sea. The coastline here had a harsh, jagged look, fashioned by the heavy seas hammering at the cliffs for thousands of years. The fuchsia hedges that lined the road were bent and twisted into tortured shapes by the fierce Atlantic wind. It was exactly the kind of wild and beautiful place Julia had imagined herself finding in Ireland. She was thrilled by the thought that they were on the very edge of Europe, that there was no other land between here and America, three thousand miles away. The ocean looked huge and unfathomable. Julia was beginning to understand why people talked about the mystic quality of the west.

Denis, however, was in a bad mood. They'd got stuck behind a tourist coach on the narrow road. It was the most restrained coach driver Denis had ever encountered, and he was forced to crawl along at twenty miles an hour. Everything began to get on his nerves. The hairstyles of the people sitting on the back seat of the coach. The dogs who dashed out into the road barking and snapping at the wheels of the car. The relentless adverts for ancient monuments — SEE THE BIGGEST BEEHIVE HUT IN KERRY!

"Beehive Huts date from the early Christian period, and are thought to have been used as religious hermitages," Julia read from the guide book.

"A rip off," replied Denis.

Even the size of the fields annoyed him.

"Why are they so small?" he'd asked, irritably. "They must be hopelessly uneconomic. It dosen't make sense. Only the Irish could come up with a system like that."

Julia, reading from the guidebook, explained how under British rule Catholics could neither buy land, nor inherit it other than by dividing it equally between all the sons.

"That's probably why you still see so many small fields here. See, there's an explanation for everything," she said.

Denis grunted and asked her if that was supposed to make him feel guilty. They'd driven on in silence until the road turned northward with the cliffs at Slea Head, revealing the desolate, rocky shapes of the Blasket Islands, a few miles off the coast. Julia had bought Peig Sayers's *Peig* in a bookshop in Cork, and had been rivetted by her description of the harsh life of the Blasket Islanders. They'd survived by fishing, and breeding a few cows. There had never been a shop, doctor or priest on the island. The last people left in 1953. Now Julia caught her breath as she saw the Blaskets for the first time, and she suggested they stop and go for a walk.

Denis wanted to keep going. He'd finally overtaken the tourist coach, after it had stopped to let the passengers visit a beehive hut, and didn't want to run the risk of getting stuck behind it again. "According to the guide book, you can see the ruins of the village at the north end of the Great Blasket," Julia paused, before adding, "With a pair of binoculars." Denis had bought a pair of binoculars before they'd come on holiday, and jumped at every opportunity to use them.

They parked the car above the strand at Slea Head and made their way along a narrow path winding up the cliff. Julia couldn't help feeling a little disappointed, the guide book had recommended stopping for a while to *Enjoy the constantly changing patterns of light on the islands and the sea*. But it was a grey, gloomy day; Julia felt drops of rain in the gusting wind and zipped up her cagoule. After they'd walked for about ten minutes, the path came to an abrupt end, blocked by a ramshackle wooden fence topped with rusty barbed wire.

Denis shook the fence angrily.

"What is this? Colditz?"

He nodded behind them.

"Let's see if we can get over that wall up there and walk down to the edge of the cliff, that's where we'll get the best view."

"Is that all that matters then? Getting the best view? Can't you just relax and *be* here?" asked Julia.

"For god's sake," muttered Denis, clutching his binoculars

and striding up the hill at a pace he knew Julia wouldn't be able to match.

Denis could see no way of getting over the dry stone wall, which was chest high, and topped by a roll of barbed wire. "Look, there are some stones sticking out, like steps, where that little girl is sitting," said Julia and started walking towards them. Denis, annoyed that his wife had discovered the way over before him, frowned and looked round for an alternative route before reluctantly following her.

Julia stared at the little girl sitting on top of the wall as she approached, wondering why she was sitting there on her own. She looked so forlorn that Julia began to feel guilty as she did whenever she passed a homeless person on the streets of London. The girl was holding herself in, trying to make herself smaller against the wind. Her long red hair was blowing out behind her, revealing a pale, freckled face and scrawny neck. The stuffing was coming out of one of the shoulders of her cheap blue anorak, and the knees of her jeans were covered in mud. She looked frozen stiff, and ready to burst into tears at any moment.

"Hello there," Julia said cheerily as she put her hands on top of the wall, just a couple of feet from the girl, and prepared to clamber up.

"It's a pound to come in," said the little girl, narrowing her eyes.

"I beg your pardon?"

Julia halted, one leg on the first stone, the other still on the ground. A look of annoyance crept into the girl's eyes and she repeated that it was a pound to come in. Julia noticed a money bag draped over the girl's shoulder for the first time. Denis caught up.

"Well? What is it now? Are you stuck?"

Julia took her foot off the stone, turned around.

"She says it's a pound to come in Denis."

"Wha-aat? Are you joking?"

The little girl, expressionless, looked into the middle distance, pulling away a strand of hair which had flicked into her eyes.

Julia took a step back and squinted to her left, "Look at this" she said, noticing for the first time a hand-painted sign. It read

Would you like a nice walk? Only £1 (50p children) to visit the most westerly point in Europe.

"This is incredible," shouted Denis, waving a hand at the sign. "Are you seriously telling me that you charge people a pound for walking across a field?"

The girl looked at Denis and spoke in a mechanical voice, as if she had said the same words countless times.

"It's private land. It belongs to my father."

"Hell's bells!"

Denis started laughing bitterly.

"I don't believe this. It's bloody outrageous."

Julia was studying the girl, trying to see beyond the stony expression and narrowed eyes. The girl must have known that Julia was staring at her, but refused to meet her eye.

Denis started walking towards the girl, hands thrust into the pockets of his cagoule, an incredulous look on his face.

"This is totally out of order. We have a perfect right to walk wherever we want. Why should we pay for the privilege? I mean, for Christ's sake, look at it."

He took a hand from his pocket and pointed at the land. It was bumpy, full of stones, a few dozen miserable looking sheep were nibbling at the windblown grass.

"It's hardly Kew Gardens, is it?"

"It's my father's land," repeated the girl.

Julia sighed, "Forget it, it's going to rain anyhow. We could always go back to Dingle and see Fungi the dolphin."

Julia had noticed a group of disabled children waiting for one of the boats which took people out to see the dolphin; contact with Fungi was reputed to be very therapeutic. Julia was longing to see him.

"Will you stop going on about that bloody stupid dolphin? It's just another way of fleecing gullible tourists. I want to go for a walk. I want to use my binoculars."

"Oh Denis, leave it. She's only doing what she's been told. For god's sake, she looks about eight years old."

"I'm ten," said the girl.

Julia, stung by the girl's icy manner, turned away, rummaged in her bag for her cigarettes and lighter. Denis watched her struggle to keep the lighter's flame working in the wind, a smile forming on his lips. Suddenly he turned back to the girl and asked, "Do you get to keep any of this money?" The girl said nothing and looked past him.

"Ten per cent plus commission I'll bet," said Denis jovially, more able to see the funny side now that Julia had lost her cool.

"Do you sit here every day?"

The girl nodded, reluctantly.

"What time do you start in the morning?"

"First thing. After my breakfast."

"And what time do you knock off?"

"When it gets dark."

"My god!" Julia shook her head, exhaling a stream of smoke. "It's no better than slavery. Someone should report your father."

Denis spluttered with laughter.

"Don't be so naive. I'll bet if we came back in a couple of hours she'd have gone home for her tea, especially on a day like this."

"I would not. I'd still be here, you'd still have to pay a pound."

Denis shook his head.

"Is that what your father taught you to say?"

"He doesn't teach me to say anything, it's the truth."

"What about when the weather's bad, like today, don't we get a discount? Look, it's going to rain any minute. I'll give you 50p for both of us."

"It's a pound."

"There's no way I'm giving you a pound, do you understand? If you keep on asking me for a pound I'm turning around and going back the way I came. Then you'll end up with nothing. So why don't you take the 50p? Go on, I'll throw in a packet of Polos, that's my final offer."

The girl shook her head. Denis took a deep breath.

"Tell me, are those a particularly rare breed of sheep? Is there a moving statue in the corner of the field? Or perhaps you're going to perform something from *Riverdance* for us? I mean, just what is it exactly that we get for our money?"

"To walk on my father's land."

Denis slapped his forehead with his hand.

"This is daylight robbery. What's so special about your father's bloody land?"

"It *is* the most westerly point in Europe, Denis," said Julia in a reasonable voice. Denis glared at her while she raised the hood on her cagoule and tied the cord around her neck, smiling to herself.

When Denis turned round again, he thought he saw the glimmer of a smile fade from the girl's face too and he raised his voice.

"So you have proof that this is the most westerly point in Europe, I presume? This is the entrance to an official site, is it? I obviously must have missed the National Trust landmark."

"This isn't England, Denis."

"God, don't I know it," he muttered. "Your father's a bit of a Renaissance Man, isn't he?" he continued. "Farmer, cartographer, sign writer, manager of a child labour scheme..."

"Denis!"

The girl was staring at him with undisguised loathing now.

"Where is the great man?" Denis nodded back the way they'd come. "Relaxing in the saloon of The Atlantic Bar?"

"Denis, stop it! This is embarrassing."

"Can't you see what's happening here? If her father was to sit there himself he wouldn't make a penny. People would take one look at him, think he was a terrible conman and tell him where to go. But when they see a little waif sitting here looking like she's one step from the poorhouse, what happens? People feel sorry for her and pay up. It's utterly cynical, nothing but emotional blackmail."

"Since when have you cared so much about children?" Julia asked with such bitterness that Denis flinched and fell silent. For a moment he resembled a trapped animal. He didn't meet her eyes, though he could feel them on him.

"Here," snapped Julia, brushing past Denis towards the girl, opening her bag and taking out her purse.

"Hey! No you don't," shouted Denis, grabbing Julia's shoulder. He snatched the purse from her hand, stuffed it into the pocket of his cagoule, then clambered up the steps and over the wall before she could snatch it back. He turned to the girl and started waving his arms and shouting at her.

"Well? What are you going to do now? Call up your father on his mobile? Have Securicor eject me?"

The girl's face was a picture of misery and fury, but it was

Julia who replied.

"You're behaving like an absolute prat Denis. If only you could see yourself."

Denis shrugged and raised his eyebrows.

"Give me my purse please."

"Come and get it. Come on, I'll take a picture of you standing on the most westerly point in Europe."

"Give... me... my... purse" Julia said through clenched teeth.

Denis started walking slowly backwards, saying "Come and get it" over and over in a teasing sing-song voice. Julia didn't reply, but slowly held out her hand. Eventually Denis came to a halt, shouted "For god's sake, can't you take a joke?" and threw the purse up into the air. It sailed in a high arc over the wall, landing on the ground a couple of feet from Julia. She bent down and picked it up, then walked over to the girl, who was still watching Denis. He'd turned his back on them now and was walking towards the sheep, kicking stones in front of him as he went. He began singing *On Ilkley Moor Bar Tat* with grim determination. Julia frowned, poked the coins around her purse with her index finger, searching for the right money.

"Here you are love."

The girl turned and regarded her sullenly. Julia held out two pound coins.

"They're English," the girl said scornfully.

"It's alright. I've seen people take them in shops."

"They're worth less than punts."

"Eh?"

"It's not enough."

Julia laughed bitterly.

"You cheeky little... my god. Well I'm not going with him, so you can keep the change. That's good business by anybody's standards, alright?"

The girl took the coins and dropped them in her money bag, moving her lips while she did so.

"What was that?" asked Julia.

"Thank you," replied the girl in a whisper, looking the other way.

Julia took a last drag from her cigarette, flicked the butt to the ground. She crossed her arms on top of the wall and rested her chin on them.

She snuck another look at the girl, who was chewing her fingernails, still staring at Denis's retreating back.

"Don't you mind sitting out here all day?" asked Julia softly. The girl shrugged.

"Don't you get lonely? I would."

Another shrug.

"My name's Julia, what's your name?"

The girl looked up into the sky, taking a sudden interest in the seagulls wheeling above them. Julia sighed, took out her cigarettes and lighter, thought better of it, put them back.

She straightened up and stepped back from the wall. When she said goodbye the girl made an almost imperceptible movement of her head which Julia decided was a nod. She'd only been walking for a little while when the shower began, the icy raindrops striking her cheeks like stones. She stopped and looked behind her. The girl sat motionless on the wall, making no effort to protect herself from the rain. Denis would be in a foul mood when he returned. He'd shrug off any attempts to discuss what had happened and would want to sit in a pub and read the English newspaper he'd bought in Dingle. She should have known it would be like this. Julia shook her head, turned round, began walking back to the car.

A HOME FROM HOME

Ewa and I left Poland shortly after martial law was declared in 1981, determined to make a fresh start here in England. We rented a gloomy ground floor flat in Hammersmith, drawn there because so many other Poles were living in that area. However the older ones soon began to depress me when I came across them in the dusty little shops off King Street, buying their bigos, Zubrowka and Wisniowka. They all had the far away look of people who had lived in their own heads for too long. It made me angry, the way they completely refused to adapt to the modern world. They preferred to dream of returning to Poland, Poland as it was thirty or forty years ago that is. That stupid dream was all they had to keep them going. We weren't going to make the same mistake.

We spent the first few weeks contacting all the other Poles whose names and addresses we'd been given. They were very kind, but every evening we had the same conversation. How popular our cause was here, how many English people wore Solidarity badges and went on demonstrations against martial law. How the West was really behind us this time. By the end of the evening we had kicked every communist out of office and restored the Polish commonwealth. I would wake up the next morning with a blinding headache, the inevitable consequence of Polish hospitality, and wonder when our new life would start.

I'd worked as a translator at home, and my English was good, if rather stiff and formal. I tried to find similar work here, offering Polish, English, Russian, Czech and German. My knowledge of German and Czech was limited to ordering two beers, but I knew all about market forces and the need to diversify. With a huge pile of dictionaries, gallons of black coffee and the desperate energy of the exile I somehow managed to complete my assignments. Gradually the work became more regular and we bought a piano so that Ewa, who had been a music teacher at home, could give lessons instead of cleaning offices. We survived.

I longed to make English friends, to be accepted here. But I soon found that being able to speak the language was not the same thing as being able to understand what people meant. Not knowing what was considered normal and what was strange, I displayed the same attitude towards anyone who engaged me in conversation — extreme gratitude. This resulted in some strange encounters. I ended up listening to a woman at a bus stop who told me how the children in her street had made her life a misery by banging on her door and throwing stones at her windows. Everyone else backed away from us as she loudly informed me that she knew the devil had sent them, having seen their tails as they ran away. Then there was the man who promised to show me something that would change my life. We walked to Ravenscourt Park, where he pointed solemnly at a patch of flattened grass which, he explained, was where the spaceship had landed. I carried on nodding and smiling as he told me how aliens had taken him back to their planet and put him on show in a zoo, before returning him to that same spot some years later unharmed, but with his eyes opened. There were many others like this, I seemed to attract them like a magnet.

Yet even when I met normal English people things seemed to go wrong. The conversation would start pleasantly enough, but at some point which I would desperately try and pinpoint for hours afterwards, I would go too far. My voice would become a little too loud, my expression a little too intense, my opinions too strong, and, before I realised it, I had stepped over some invisible threshold. Ewa felt it too. She said "I feel I have to pretend nothing matters, otherwise I frighten people."

But for a certain kind of English person we were not without interest. Felicity was an attractive, well bred woman, who seemed intrigued by Poland. She wanted to know all about the queues for food, the secret police, my underground activities. Ewa and I had sheltered people on the run, passed on messages, daubed slogans on walls, no more nor less than everyone else we knew. What was there to talk about?

Yet the more I denied having played any significant part in

opposing the state, the more alluring she seemed to find me, convinced that I was being unduly modest. I can't pretend that I wasn't flattered.

She invited me to tea at her house in Primrose Hill. Her mouth formed a beautiful, silent 'O' when I presented her with a bunch of flowers on the doorstep. She seemed charmed by what she obviously took to be a quaint, un-English gesture, but then gently scolded me for acting like a chauvinist. I, on the other hand, couldn't understand what all the fuss was about, in Poland one doesn't visit without bringing flowers. In Felicity's hallway hung a framed poster for Wajda's *Man Of Iron*, together with others supporting the Sandinistas and the ANC. In the living room beautiful Indian paintings, Moroccan pottery, an elaborately decorated hookah. Her mournful eyed spaniel, Leo, stared at me as I sat on the sofa while Felicity made the tea. She returned with the tray of tea and biscuits, just as I was poking my tongue out at it. "Leo obviously finds you fascinating too," she said, smiling as she put down the tray.

We drank several cups of what Felicity told me was almond tea while we discussed recent events in Eastern Europe. She placed her hand on my knee whilst questioning me about the prospects for Solidarity. Out of the corner of my eye I noticed the dog watching us with eager anticipation. I put my hand on Felicity's cheek and drew her mouth to mine. We rolled onto the floor, scattering china cups and saucers, grinding chocolate biscuits into the carpet. Leo saw his chance and pounced too, gratefully gobbling up the broken biscuits. Even in the midst of my passion I felt annoyed about that miserable dog getting all the biscuits and I managed to give it a kick as I struggled with the zip on my hostess's jeans. Afterwards, seeing me out, she held my face in her long, slim hands and said "I can see why they never broke your spirit." I still can't decide if she was laughing at me.

I had tea at Felicity's house several times a week for the next couple of months. This, I was certain, was the beginning of my acceptance into English society. Then one rainy Tuesday afternoon I received no answer to my ring on the doorbell. Perhaps an Englishman would have shrugged his shoulders and dismissed it as a misunderstanding, but being a Pole I immediately thought the worst. I hid inside a phonebox further down the street. After a while I saw Felicity open her door and kiss another man goodbye. He was about my age, tall, very handsome, with jet black hair and olive skin. The only thing that spoilt the film star image was the walking stick that he leant on so heavily as he made his way down the street. Later I learnt he'd recently arrived in this country after spending several years in one of General Pinochet's grimmer jails and was writing a book about his experience.

I returned home in a foul mood. As I pushed open the living room door, I discovered Ewa and a young Englishman sitting stiffly at the piano, both smiling grotesquely at me. Two half empty glasses of wine and a box of expensive chocolates stood on top of the piano. Ewa's blouse was unbuttoned, there was lipstick on the Englishman's nose. The three of us stared at each other in astonishment. A dreadful silence slowly filled the room, like water rising to the ceiling. Then, at last, I realised they were waiting for me to do something.

I walked over to the piano, stood next to the Englishman and began playing a few discordant notes. "As you can see, I have never learnt to play myself," I said, in a regretful tone of voice. "But I'm certain that if my wife had given me lessons like these, I would be a concert pianist by now. Or at least, a very happy man."

The Englishman began blushing, Ewa squirmed uncomfortably on the seat next to him. "You have adapted very well to capitalism Ewa," I continued. "It didn't take you very long to make the most of your talents. Tell me, how many other special pupils do you have?"

Ewa sprang to her feet, "Enough! Enough of these stupid games."

We began trading insults in Polish over the head of the bewildered Englishman. While I shouted, I stabbed a piano key over and over with my finger. Suddenly Ewa slammed down the lid. I withdrew my hand just in time but the Englishman, whose hands had remained frozen on the keys since I entered, was not so lucky. He screamed in agony as his fingers were trapped. Our upstairs neighbour started hammering on the ceiling, shouting "Stop that bloody row or I'll call the police. You're not in bloody Istanbul now, you noisy bastards!"

Ewa insisted on us taking the Englishman to casualty in a taxi, even though there was clearly nothing broken. I sat with him while Ewa rang his family. He flinched when I offered him a cigarette. When Ewa returned and asked him if he'd like us to stay with him till his mother arrived, he begged us to leave him alone and burst into tears.

As we stood at the bus top outside the hospital I punished Ewa with my silence. Punished her for betraying me, for making me feel guilty about Felicity, for not being able to feel at ease here. Eventually she turned to me and said "I could smell her on you weeks ago."

We didn't say a word on the journey back. It started to rain when we got off the bus; Ewa looked down at the glistening pavement and said, "I don't want to go back to the flat."

A sodden newspaper lay on the ground in front of me, *The Cork Weekly Examiner*. I remembered passing an Irish pub nearby, where somebody was playing the accordion. It was a stirring tune and I'd wanted to go in, sit in the warmth and light and listen to it properly. But I'd lost my nerve and walked on.

"I know somewhere" I said.

We found an empty seat in the corner. I stood at the bar waiting to be served, surrounded by men whose faces had disappointment and loneliness etched into them as deeply as tribal marks. The jukebox played only the saddest of songs. I began to sink into a comforting melancholy.

Ewa and I began to talk, halfway through our first drink. She told me how the pale young man from Acton had found her Slavic features and haughty manner irresistible. She was lonely. He brought her flowers, Belgian chocolates, a piano shaped brooch.

"He wanted to make me happy, can you believe it? A boy of twenty thought he could make me happy."

I touched her hand, staring at her delicate fingers;"This woman had a little dog," I said. "It looked so depressed all the time. I could never bear to have a dog with a face like that in the house. The only thing that cheered it up was chocolate biscuits." I turned and looked at her. She hadn't been listening, she was staring at a man with a battered drinker's face shoving coin after coin into the jukebox. I withdrew my hand and drained my glass. It seemed we had survived.

It was a long time before Ewa and I began to feel comfortable with each other again. Sometimes I felt that we only stayed together because neither of us had any alternative. I'm sure she felt the same, but she never said so; we played a game instead. She argued that in fact I was the one who'd had a real affair; the English boy didn't count. She hadn't desired him, rather she felt that it was her duty to teach me a lesson by taking him for a lover, there had been no pleasure in it. This was a typical piece of Ewa logic. Nevertheless it was a clever strategy, as it both relieved her of any blame and flattered me; I had remained the centre of her universe even when she was being pawed by her pupil.

Eventually she decided I'd been taught a lesson and forgave me, but the tension between us remained. Sometimes after we'd made love I would be gripped by panic. I would seem to be both there with Ewa and, at the same time, years ahead in the future, looking back, and mourning the loss of that moment. One rainy afternoon as we lay in bed, I took her in my arms and asked her to sing to me.

"Sing something that you sang when you were a girl."

She sang about a girl who loved a proud boy. The boy told the girl that he loved her too. He wanted them to have the best wedding feast anyone had ever seen. But he was poor, he could only afford bread. The girl told him that she didn't care how grand their wedding feast was, the only thing that mattered to her was their love for each other. But the boy wouldn't listen, for him it had to be the best or nothing. He travelled far away to earn his fortune. He wrote often, telling her how well he was doing and promising that soon he would be sending for her to come and join him and be his wife. After a while the letters stopped. She learnt that he had married the daughter of a rich lord. She died lonely and broken hearted.

When she finished we lay together in silence, listening to the rain drumming against the window, the drone and swish of traffic on the wet road.

"Are you happy?" I asked her.

"It's so long since you asked me that."

"Are you?"

She turned her face to the pillow.

"Don't keep asking me."

"I want to know."

"Ask me something else."

I ran my hand gently across her shoulder, reached out and pushed her hair behind her ear; "Sing to me."

She pushed me away, gently raised herself up on the pillows.

"Taduesz, you have to find something new."

I asked her what she meant. I could see that she was annoyed she had to explain, I'm supposed to understand riddles immediately.

"You're slipping away. Half the time you're not here with me at all, you're," she waved her hand in frustration, "somewhere else completely."

"Yes! Thinking about work. I work like a dog, in case you hadn't noticed."

"No, no, I don't mean that. You're not living, you're thinking about how difficult life is. Something has to change, you must change, otherwise... I don't know what, I really don't."

Shortly after this conversation I received a depressing letter from my parents in Poland. Things were very bad at home. My mother spent hours queuing in the freezing cold for food, my father's heart condition had grown worse and there was a lack of medical supplies. I feared the worst. One night I woke suddenly, certain that something terrible had happened. I thought about ringing my parents, to reassure myself, but then dismissed the idea as stupid and melodramatic.

Taking care not to wake Ewa, I got up, went into the kitchen and poured myself a large glass of vodka. Then another, and another, till the dreadful anxiety was slowly replaced by a warm, floating feeling. I began to see the funny side of things.

Remembering how our English neighbours thought we were Turks, I burst out laughing.

When I was on my fourth or fifth glass I noticed the time, it was three a.m. Without thinking, I held my breath and listened.

When I didn't hear anything, I felt a terrible emptiness. It took me a few moments to work out exactly what sound I'd been expecting — the bugle call from the clock tower of Mariacki church, in the market place at home in Cracow.

During the Tartar raids hundreds of years ago, the watchman positioned there saw the invaders approaching and took up his bugle to raise the alarm. His warning was cut short by an arrow piercing his throat, and the Tartars destroyed Cracow, one of the most beautiful cities in Europe. Ever since, on the hour, every hour, a bugler plays that same haunting melody, stopping suddenly at the exact same point the watchman was killed. Even the communists had not dared interfere with this tradition.

Sometimes when I was a boy, I would wake in the middle of the night and hear the sound of the bugle drifting across the grey, rusting roof tops. In the early hours especially, when everything is so quiet and still, it has a beautiful, thrilling clarity. When I listened to it, my own sadness was absorbed into a greater one and became easier to bear. But that night, the only sounds were the occasional drone of a car passing by on the Hammersmith flyover, or the muffled sounds of the old man who lived on his own next door, calling out in his sleep.

The kitchen door opened and Ewa came in hesitantly, screwing up her eyes against the light. She held her dressing gown closed tightly around her neck with one hand, ran her hand through her hair with the other.

"What's the matter?" she asked.

I shrugged.

"I felt like a drink."

She sighed, slowly shook her head, "Come on, what is it?"

"I was certain something bad had happened at home. Have you ever felt that?"

She frowned, said "Yes, many times," then walked over, picked up the bottle and poured herself a drink.

"Ewa?"

She sipped the vodka, looking down at the floor, her knuckles whitening where she gripped her dressing gown.

"Do you think we were right to leave?"

"This kind of question isn't healthy. Now we're here we have to make the most of it."

"But ..."

"You must be strong."

"I don't understand how things work here."

"You understood well enough to get yourself an English

mistress."

"While you resisted temptation."

She looked away. For a moment I thought she was going to cry, but suddenly she drained her glass, sighed and said "Shall we go back to bed now?"

We were spending too much time in the flat together, that much was clear. I embarked on a new routine. In Poland hiking is a national passion. In the spring Ewa and I would get the bus to Zakopane and spend a weekend roaming the Tatra mountains. That beautiful countryside had entered my soul and become a part of me. I hoped that by exploring London thoroughly on foot I would absorb some of the spirit of this great city. Every morning I got up at six, my head still swimming with words from yesterday's translation, had breakfast, then set off. I walked through Battersea Park and Hyde Park, over Hammersmith Bridge, through the leafy streets of Barnes, on to Putney Heath and Wimbledon Common. Then west to Gunnersby Park, along the river to Chiswick, Syon Park and Twickenham.

On the way back I would stop for a drink, to reward myself for my efforts. But I never managed to feel comfortable in any of the places that I tried. If the pub was very quiet, I imagined that everyone had been offended by my presence, if there was laughter I felt sure that it was at my expense.

I had to admit that English people still baffled me. For instance, whenever I asked someone how they were, they'd smile triumphantly and reply "Very well, thank you", flaunting their good fortune and well being, as if life was a bed of roses and only fools did not have a wonderful time. Or else they would say "musn't grumble", as if it were a crime to talk of the obvious cruelties and injustices of life.

Slowly I realised that the only place I really felt at ease was in the Irish pub. Before long I began to receive barely perceptible nods from the regulars as I entered, and the barman would raise his finger in acknowledgement. I liked the barman, his usual expression was one of curious expectation, as if he was always listening to a lengthy, but ultimately amusing joke. We exchanged a few words about the weather while he pulled my drink, and I enjoyed watching the stout stand there, calming itself, while he served another customer, before returning to fill the glass completely and hand it to me with a nod.

The pub's plainness, its transitory atmosphere, also appealed to me. The other pubs I tried had been made to resemble the inside of someone's house, with their thick carpets, fake beams, and paintings of country scenes on the walls. The carpet in the Irish pub was threadbare, there were no paintings on the wall, the tables were shiny and worn. It suited me fine. There were rarely any women there, and I had the feeling that most of the customers led rather lonely lives; that this was one of the few places where they could gain comfort.

I began to recognise the songs on the jukebox, and always made sure I had some change so that I could play my favourites. I particularly liked *Paddy's Green Shamrock Shore*, *My Love Is In America*, and *The Town I Loved So Well*. Listening to these sad songs eased my own sadness.

One day when Ewa had no pupils I persuaded her to come out walking with me. I wanted to show her how well I knew London, and took pride in guiding her through the side streets and along the river to the Royal Botanic Gardens at Kew, where we spent the afternoon. On the way back, we stopped in the Irish pub.

It was early evening, the bar was barely half full. I was aware of everyone looking at Ewa with curiosity. They were used to seeing me on my own. The one occasion that we had gone there together before, the pub was noisy and crowded and no one took much notice of us. The barman asked me if Ewa was an actress when he handed me my change. I laughed, "All Polish women are actresses."

When I returned with the drinks, Ewa looked around her with an ironic expression on her face.

"So this is where you come every day. Such elegance!"

I shrugged, "It's OK."

Just then the barman looked at his watch, reached up and turned on the television perched on the wall at the end of the bar. My heart sank as I realised he planned to watch the news. That whole day Ewa and I had avoided talking about it.

The first few items aroused little interest, people carried on chatting and laughing, barely glancing up at the screen. Then came the report of Jerzy Popieluszko's funeral — the Solidarity priest who'd been beaten to death by the police. I caught an old man staring at Ewa and me as we both instinctively made the sign of the cross. Ewa reached for my hand. The barman's usual expression of ironic amusement changed to one of intense interest, and he reached up and increased the volume. Everyone's eyes were suddenly drawn to the pictures of the huge funeral procession making its way through the grey streets. The place fell completely silent, the only voice heard in the room was that of the reporter. The camera went into a close up of Jerzy's elderly parents, weeping as they watched his coffin being lowered into the ground. Ewa could contain herself no longer. Jumping to her feet she shouted "Murderers!" at the top of her voice. I looked around at the astonished faces. In all the time I had been going there, I had been very careful never to raise my voice or drawn attention to myself. Yet within minutes of her arrival, Ewa was creating a scene. Gesturing at the pictures on the television she cried, "Where will it end? How long before we get justice?"

I could feel everyone staring at us as she sat back down. I squeezed Ewa's hand, but part of me silently cursed her for embarrassing me in the one place I felt comfortable. They moved onto another story, the barman turned the sound down again, but no one spoke, something had changed in the room.

The barman walked over holding two large whiskies, put them down on the table in front of us and said, "They're on the house."

By the time I had recovered enough to say thank you, he was already walking back to the bar. He switched off the television, saying "That's enough bad news for one day. How about giving us a tune Eamon?" An old man pulled an accordion from under his chair. As soon as he started playing I recognised the tune. For some reason it seemed terribly important, I turned and said to Ewa, "This is it! This is the tune I heard when I first walked past. This is the one."

She patted my hand absently. I couldn't find the words to explain to her that I now understood this music, that she too, if she tried, could appreciate the sorrow, anger, and defiance that it contained. It was like the Polish spirit. This kind of music could only have come out of great loss and suffering, could only have been composed by someone who understood how desperately cruel life could be.

A rough looking fellow in working clothes approached us. He was painfully shy, and fiddled with his ear while he spoke.

"That's a terrible thing they did... murdering that priest."

I thanked him for his concern. His eyes kept wandering nervously over to Ewa. She smiled and asked him to join us.

"Ah no, I wouldn't want to disturb you."

Ewa reached out and gently touched his sleeve, "Please."

He blushed. To save his embarrassment, I asked him where he came from. He cleared his throat noisily and, continuing to stand awkwardly at the edge of our table, told us about his home in Cork, how he'd had to leave because there was no work there. He lived a nomadic existence, working on building sites here, in Germany and Holland. The Irish, he said, were used to travelling, once they had travelled to escape oppression, now they travelled because there was not enough work for them in Ireland. Or maybe because it had simply become a habit they couldn't shake off. He shrugged, then took a long drink from his glass. We introduced ourselves, his name was Liam.

The tune finished, I applauded warmly, someone shouted "Good man Eamon!" The old man acknowledged the cry, took a swig from his pint, then started playing another tune.

"When I was in school," said Liam, "The teachers were always telling us what a fantastic country Poland was. 'The Poles are queuing up to be priests' they said, 'you youngsters should take a leaf out of their book. If the Irish had their faith, we'd soon get this country back on its feet.' Ah yes, Poland is a great place."

I insisted on buying Liam a drink. While I waited to be served I looked around at the other customers. They too had not managed to fit in here, they too were burdened with painful memories of their homeland. A man in front of me indicated to the barman that I should be served next. The others stood aside to create more room. I was deeply moved by these strangers extending the hand of friendship to me on such a terrible day. I had found a home from home.

HAPPY HOURS

On Wednesdays all drinks were a £1 between six and nine at The Prince Of Wales. Nicky and Colin got there at twenty past six, found a table well away from the jukebox and fruit machine. Nicky looked around at all the other unemployed, middle-aged men soaking up the cheap booze.

"I'm sick of this place."

Colin looked up from his pint.

"It's not so bad."

"It's a dump," said Nicky pressing his hand on the edge of the table, making it wobble.

"Don't."

"The tables are all like this. The stuffing's coming out of the seats... the stuffing's coming out of most of the bloody customers. I'd just like to go somewhere decent for a change, that's all."

Colin was carefully folding the beermat into a wedge.

"Where? Like The Westgate you mean?"

"No, not The Westgate. They're a right snotty crowd up there."

Colin bent down and pushed the folded beermat under one of the legs, pressed his hand on the edge of the table.

"There!"

"Brilliant."

Nicky took a long swig from his pint, shut his eyes, sighed.

"Christ, I needed that."

"What's up?"

"I've had one of those days."

"Yeah?"

"Yeah."

Colin waited for him to say something else, but Nicky just stared at the flashing lights of the fruit machine. He dropped it, he knew Nicky too well.

Nicky took out his tin of tobacco, started rolling a cigarette. He was gasping, hadn't had one since the morning, to prove to himself he could do without if he wanted. He glanced at a poster for the pub quiz night on Thursday. He used to enjoy that. Him, Colin and Paul would come every week. Everyone on their team had been made redundant. All newcomers were greeted with *Come to join the scrapheap, have you?* Paul was really into it, he was always in the library reading up reference books. He was their top scorer. He had a sharp mind, he could have gone far if he'd tried harder at school, no doubt about it.

Then there was Colin, Christ, you had to laugh sometimes. The things he came out with.

What subject did Mr Chips teach?

Cookery?

Sometimes, if people laughed, he'd get flustered, start to panic, and come out with complete rubbish.

What's the capital of Canada?

Melvyn Bragg.

Why don't you go do something useful, and go get a round in, Colin?

The trouble was, it always turned into an expensive evening, what with the drinks, fags, crisps and nuts, plus the raffle tickets for some charity they always flogged in the interval. Now they limited themselves to times like these, Happy Hours, special offers.

"You should get an allotment," said Colin. "Whenever things start to get on top of me, I always go and spend an hour on my allotment."

Jesus, the last thing he wanted was a bloody allotment. He only had to look at something green for it to shrivel up and die.

What am I going to do? The doctor's told me I've only got a year to live.

Get yourself an allotment. Then it'll feel like twenty.

Colin drummed his fingers on the table.

"Paul's late."

Nicky searched his pockets for matches. He wished Colin wouldn't drum his fingers like that.

"He's usually here first."

"Uh huh."

Nicky found his matches, lit his cigarette, watching an old

man pour beer into the empty ashtray on his table. When it was full he carefully picked it up and placed it on the floor for his Jack Russell to drink. The man smiled as he watched his dog greedily lap it up. Probably the only friend he's got left, the poor old sod, thought Nicky. He hoped to Christ he didn't end up like that.

"I wonder if Paul's alright," said Colin, in a tone of voice that made it obvious that he wanted Nicky to reassure him that he was.

"I don't know. Why don't you ring up The Royal Gwent and see if he's been admitted to Casualty?"

Colin's face went tight, he looked away and reached for his pint. Damn. Nicky felt like a prick. It had come out all wrong, he'd meant it as a joke, but he'd ended up sounding really nasty. There was an awkward silence.

Colin was a good mate but he got on Nicky's nerves sometimes, the way he kept on asking stupid questions like a little kid. Usually he managed to make a joke out of it. But sometimes he just wasn't in the mood for it, like tonight.

Nicky had been in a bad mood all day. That morning he and Maureen had had a row about housework. It was really a continuation of the row they'd started the night before, when Maureen had come home from work and had a go at him for not having done the washing up.

"You've had nothing to do all day, and you couldn't even manage to wash a few dishes."

She'd been getting at him ever since she'd started working, a couple of months ago. Sian their youngest was in the room, pretending to watch *Brookside*, but taking in every word. He couldn't believe Maureen could say something like that in front of her. He told Sian to go upstairs and do her homework.

"I don't have any."

"Go upstairs!"

She stomped out, slamming the door behind her. It was a joke really, making Sian leave the room, she probably heard every word anyway. The argument wasn't really about housework, it was about the fact that Maureen had a job and he didn't, they both knew that.

She'd been quick off the mark when it came to getting that job in the new Tesco's down in Maesglas mind, fair play. She'd read a story in *The Argus* about how customers had walked out in disgust when there was no one old enough on the checkouts to serve them booze. The place was packed with sixteen and seventeen-year olds. Maureen and her friend Janet had gone down there the next morning and asked if there were any vacancies for mature women.

But it wasn't just the fact that she was the one earning the money that got to Nicky. It was the little things, like the way she always had plenty of stories to tell when she came home — about what her workmates got up to behind the scenes, or the stupid things the customers said.

And him?

I signed on today. The queue wasn't too bad. I had a look in the job-centre after, but there was nothing there. I went over to Paul's and we had a game of cards, then took the dog for a walk. He nearly got in a fight with another dog, but Paul grabbed him just in time.

Sometimes he made things up rather than say nothing — a woman's carrier bag bursting open, spilling her shopping all over the pavement, and a dog running off with her sausages. A drunk caught in a revolving door. Anything to get a smile out of her.

As she was letting herself out of the front door, Maureen turned to him.

"You're letting yourself go Nicky. You used to be a smart-looking bloke. Full of life, you were. Now you just sit around moping all day. I know it's hard being out of work, but you've got to try and do something with yourself before it's too late. I know you think I'm nagging but... "

She shook her head wearily, and left without finishing.

You're letting yourself go.

There was nothing wrong with him, he was in good nick for his age. All the same, he was on edge, he needed to get out of the house, find something to take his mind off things. He decided to take a walk up town, going the long way round, cutting through the playing fields to Cardiff Road, down to the roundabout, up through Belle Vue Park (very steep there — good exercise), then down Stow Hill into the centre.

You're letting yourself go.

He went into The Body Shop and looked at the men's section. £8 for a little bottle of aftershave! Who in god's name would pay that much? It was amazing, some of the things blokes bought these days. Little black bags for carrying your shaving gear that looked like women's handbags. What next? Mud soap! He burst out laughing and the woman next to him inspecting a natural sponge clicked her tongue and walked away. The young shop assistant was looking at him anxiously, as if she was worried he might break something, as if he was too clumsy to be left wandering around on his own in there. Pretty though. A good figure on her, and he liked the way she wore her hair piled up high, like Audrey Hepburn.

The snotty woman walked up to the counter and handed the shop assistant the sponge. When she bent down to get a bag he stared at her breasts, hanging down in her low top. Christ they were lovely. He couldn't take his eyes off them. He felt himself growing hard. Then she came up suddenly, caught him staring, and looked away, embarrassed. He felt himself blushing. What was he thinking of? She couldn't have been much older than Sian. The snotty one was giving him a filthy look. He put the mud soap back and got out of there as fast as he could.

Going past another shop, he caught his reflection in the mirror. Unshaven, greasy hair, fat gut, the same old clothes. A girl like her would run a mile from him.

You're letting yourself go.

He walked over to the reference library. All the newspapers were taken, so he started looking through an Encyclopedia while he waited.

Majorca, Menorca and Ibiza are the most famous of The Balearic Islands.

That was worth remembering, that kind of question often came up in pub quizzes. Perhaps they should start going again? It would sharpen up the brain. Help stop the rot setting in. Why not? He could make a pint last all evening if he wanted to, just the way he was cutting down on the fags. He'd suggest it to Paul. No need to tell Colin. He checked on the name of a few capital cities while he was at it.

Five, ten minutes passed, but no one returned a paper. It was so stuffy in there. How could they bear it?

Italy is the world's top wine producer.

Funny, he thought it would have been France. That was interesting too.

He looked up again. The bastards were going to hang on to those papers all bloody day. Some of them weren't really reading them at all. They were yawning, scratching themselves, picking their noses. What a bloody shower. He'd give it five more minutes. Nicky turned away, flicked through some more pages, came across a table estimating the most frequent cancers worldwide. Christ, no thanks. His scalp began to itch, he felt a dull, throbbing pain in his head. He looked up again and saw someone folding up *The Mirror*. At last! But a young bloke shot in ahead of him.

"Excuse me mate. Have you finished with that?"

"Yes mate, here you are."

Bastard!

He rammed the encyclopedia back on the shelves with such force that everyone turned and stared. He had to get out of there quick, before he exploded. He pushed past the newspaper hoarders, knocking a broadsheet out of someone's hands.

"Hey! Watch where you're going."

He looked down into the man's startled face.

"Fuck off!"

The man's mouth dropped open. When he reached the door, Nicky turned round and shouted at the top of his voice, "You can stick your newspapers up your arses."

He pushed open the doors, and ran down the stairs out into John Frost Square. He stood by the entrance to the library, heart thumping. Jesus, what had come over him? He'd never done anything like that before. Acting like a raving bloody madman, he was. That was it, he could never go back there again now. He started rolling a fag. His hands were trembling. He began taking deep breaths.

"Come on now, Nicky, there's nothing the matter with you. Don't be soft man."

The panic gradually began to die down. He felt better outside, surrounded by noise and movement. He lit up, then wandered into the square. He had no idea where he was going, he just needed to walk. Then he noticed something unusual going on at the far end of the square.

Nicky realised that he did have something to tell Colin after all.

"I saw a couple of llamas in John Frost Square this morning."

Colin squinted at him suspiciously.

"Very funny."

He was still pissed off at him. Nicky leaned over and gently nudged him.

"Straight up. They were in a pen, it was part of this exhibition about a wildlife park."

Colin was interested now.

"Really? What were they like?"

"Ugly looking buggers. They've got this way of looking down their noses at you, as if they're saying *Who do you think you are, you peasant?*"

Nicky half-closed his eyes, stretched out his neck and looked down his nose at Colin.

"Like that."

Colin started laughing. Nicky turned round and tried his llama impression on the Jack Russell. It started growling at him. Colin snorted, some beer went up his nose.

"Do you know who they reminded me of when they did that?"

Colin shook his head. He was grinning, he really wanted to know. Nicky leaned back, flicked some ash off the end of his fag.

"Prince Philip."

They burst out laughing. Colin said, "That'd be the day, wouldn't it? If they stuck Phil in a pen in John Frost Square."

"Aye, I'll drink to that."

They raised their glasses.

"Cheers!"

"Cheers!"

They started thinking of all the other people they'd like to see put in a pen.

"Thatcher."

"No, it wouldn't be fair."

"Why not?"

"She'd frighten the kiddies."

The list grew longer and longer. By the end they were wiping the tears from their eyes. Nicky was feeling better now. There was nothing like getting out and having a few pints and a laugh with your mates. He'd been looking forward to this all day. Being out of work wouldn't be quite so bad if you could afford to go out more often and let off steam.

They'd nearly finished their pints.

"Another?" asked Colin.

"Aye, go on."

"It's funny the way they still call it Happy Hour, isn't it?"

"Eh?"

"The sign outside, it says *Every Wednesday, Happy Hour 6 till 9.*"

"So what?"

"That's three hours. It should be Happy *Hours* really."

"That's a very interesting point Colin. Now, go get the drinks."

Just then Paul walked in, winked at them, began sauntering over. Nicky noticed how many people looked up as he walked past.

It was a walk that said *No one here needs to tell me the score.* You'd never guess he'd been out of work for three years, ever since their factory had closed down. When he reached their table, he pointed his index finger at their glasses.

"My round."

"No, you're alright, I was just..."

"No, I'll get them."

Colin tried to say something else, but Paul was already walking towards the bar. Nicky felt on top form again. The row with Maureen, the empty hours kicking around the centre, getting off on the wrong foot with Colin, all that was behind him now. It was going to be a good night. Just the three of them, no wives, no kids. Nicky reminded himself to have a word with Paul about the two of them going to the quiz night again, when they were on their own.

Paul brought over three pints.

"Cheers mate."

"Hang on, I haven't finished."

He went back to the bar, brought over three whiskies and sat down.

"Bloody hell," said Colin.

Nicky looked up at Paul.

"Thanks mate... what's the occasion?"

"I've got a job, I start next week."

Nicky was stunned. It felt like someone had slapped him in the face.

"Congratulations," said Colin, in a weak voice.

"Yeah, well done mate," said Nicky, trying to sound pleased. Paul looked at him and Colin anxiously, picked up his glass of whisky and held it up in front of him. They stared at him blankly.

"Well?"

They caught on, picked up their glasses.

"Cheers!"

"Here's to you."

Paul leaned forward.

"No, here's to the three of us."

Nicky felt himself choking up. He forced himself to smile and knocked back the whisky in one. No one knew what to say next. They twirled the empty glasses in their hands, looking down at the table. Eventually Colin asked, "What's the job then?"

Paul looked embarassed.

"Security guard."

Nicky couldn't bring himself to look at him.

"Where?" asked Colin.

"St David's Shopping Centre."

"Cardiff!"

"Yeah, well, you gotta go where the work is. It won't take long on the bike."

Nicky caught Paul's eye, but he quickly looked away and picked up his pint. How could he forget what he'd said so quickly? He and Paul had gone to the St David's Shopping Centre at the end of last year, to try and do some Christmas shopping. A huge, soulless place, packed so tight you could hardly move. Awful piped Christmas carols played at a deafening volume. Angry mothers slapped whining kids. People stepped on each other, hauled shopping trolleys over each other's feet in their frenzy to find an inch of space. After a few minutes, Nicky and Paul had had enough.

"Let's get out of here before I go mad."

Making for the exit, they came across a drunk, leaning against the door of a card shop. He was singing along to *Rudolph the Red-Nosed Reindeer* at the top of his voice, a can of lager in his hand, dressed in a Welsh rugby shirt and jeans, a Santa hat on his head. His coat probably lay on the floor of some pub, along with any presents he'd bought before hitting the booze. A crowd had gathered round him, smiling and nudging each other. People had stopped going into the shop, stood outside watching him instead. Nicky and Paul joined them.

"At least he's happy," said a frazzled-looking middle-aged woman, clutching two enormous shopping bags.

"Aye, he's got the right idea alright," replied Paul, grinning.

The only one who hadn't looked happy was the manager of the card shop, who was standing inside the deserted shop, arms folded, staring daggers at the drunk.

He finished singing *Rudolph the Red-Nosed Reindeer*. The crowd applauded.

"Bravo!" shouted Paul.

The drunk took a bow. The manager angrily pushed open the door and tapped him on the shoulder.

"Excuse me."

The drunk, startled, staggered sideways.

"You're blocking my entrance."

The drunk screwed up his eyes, frowned, then took a step forward.

"Have you seen Dougie and Cath? I lost them in the market."

People laughed.

"Could you please..."

The drunk suddenly threw his arm around the manager, thrust the can of lager towards his reddening face.

"Have a drink! Go on man, lighten up for Christ's sake."

The manager tried to squirm out of the drunk's grip. A couple of young shop assistants pressed their faces against the door, enjoying their manager's embarrassment.

"I need some assistance. Over here!" the manager shouted at two passing security guards. They pushed their way through the laughing crowd.

"Come on now mate, you've had enough. Can you leave please."

"Leave him alone, he's doing no harm," said Paul.

One of the security guards turned round and gave Paul a

look.

The drunk floundered.

"What's the matter, officers?"

The manager scampered back inside to the safety of his shop. The guards persuaded the drunk to leave. As the three of them passed, Paul said, "It's bloody pissing down outside. You're full of the Christmas spirit, aren't you? I hope you're proud of yourselves."

The security guard who'd looked at him before turned and said, "Look mate, I've got no choice in the matter. I'm just doing my job."

"Wrong," said Paul. "You have got a choice. I'm unemployed, but I'd sooner go hungry than do what you're doing."

For a moment it looked as though it was going to turn nasty, but the other guard nudged his mate.

"Come on, let's go, we haven't got time for this."

They disappeared into the crowd. The other shoppers who'd been watching turned away and went about their business.

"They're paid to keep the riff-raff out," said Paul. "Now it's drunks and noisy teenagers and tramps. In a few years it'll be the likes of you and me. The unemployed, pensioners — they'll run a check on your credit value before they let you in to their precious bloody shopping centre."

"I could never do a job like that," said Nicky.

"No, nor me," said Paul.

"So, you're no longer a man of leisure," said Colin, clapping his hands together.

"That's right. I'm afraid that's the end of our afternoon card games Nicky."

Nicky shrugged.

"Ah well, I've been thinking of getting a Leisure Card and going to the baths in the afternoon, or maybe doing one of those exercise classes."

He patted his stomach,

"It's about time I got myself back in shape."

He smiled at Paul.

"You dirty bugger, you just want to ogle all those women in their leotards."

Paul laughed, a little too loud.

Nicky wished he knew how to stop feeling so angry with Paul. It was as if he'd done something underhand. Secretly Nicky always had a feeling he'd be the first one to find work. The three of them had always shared any news about decent vacancies they'd seen or heard about. But Paul had kept quiet about this. Maybe he'd been too embarrassed to admit it, perhaps he'd simply decided it was time he struck out on his own. How many other jobs had he applied for that he hadn't told them about? He could just see Maureen's face when he told her, see her thinking *if he can get a job, why can't you?*

He couldn't believe Paul had taken a job as a security guard. Still, perhaps there were things Nicky didn't know about. Maybe he was more in debt than he'd let on. It couldn't have been easy for him to tell them. At the end of the day he was still his best mate. He must have had his reasons. He'd tell him in his own time, some night when Colin wasn't there. He shouldn't judge him too harshly, he didn't know all the facts.

Nicky tried to think of something to say. But the harder he tried, the more panicky he felt. Colin started drumming his fingers on the table again. Suddenly Paul stood up.

"I'm going for a slash."

"Keep an eye out for anything suspicious," said Nicky.

"Eh?"

"You know, someone loitering, or any bags left unattended. You'll have to be security conscious from now on."

Paul looked at him warily, wondering if he was taking the piss. Then he winked and pointed at him as if he was a right wag.

"Oh aye, right."

Nicky buried his face in his pint. What a pathetic attempt at a joke. When Paul had gone, Colin said, "You'll have to tell him about the llamas."

"Aye."

Nicky brought out his tin of tobacco again and started rolling another cigarette.

"It won't be the same, will it?"

Nicky shook his head. He didn't want to think about it. He looked over at the old man, staring into space. His Jack Russell lay at his feet, licking its lips.

"How long was it we worked together?"

"Eighteen years."

Paul was Sian's godfather. The three of them and their families had gone to Spain for their summer holidays six, seven years in a row. Good times.

"It'll be odd next week, won't it? Just the two of us. Do you want to try somewhere else for a change."

"Eh?"

"Shall we go somewhere else next week?"

Nicky shook his head.

"No, this place is as good as any."

WAITING

It had been going on for months. All the neighbours knew, Zoe could tell from their looks. Looks that said *We know what your Gareth is up to with that Dinah down the road.*

Every night he came home around ten, strolled into the front room, blowing out his cheeks.

"I'm back! Fancy a drink?"

Just like that, as if everything was normal.

She'd shake her head, turn back to her book.

"Well, I think I'll have one."

He'd get a can of lager from the fridge, drink it in the kitchen listening to the radio, whistling a jaunty tune.

There was something not quite right here. Didn't she have the right to be told a plausible lie? Wasn't that part of the deal? She felt like suggesting a suitable night class: *Starting an Affair — Level One (Beginners).*

Her one attempt at confrontation had failed miserably. It was Sunday morning, she was cleaning the bath. Suddenly anger surged through her.

I can't stand another moment of this pretence.

She rushed downstairs.

"Gareth, is there somebody else?"

He looked up to see her standing in the doorway, fists clenched, a demented look in her eyes. He switched off the hoover.

"Sorry, what did you say?"

He looked as guileless and vulnerable as a labrador. How could she ever have suspected him? Tears sprang to her eyes.

"Zoe, are you alright?"

She nodded her head, fled upstairs.

"I warned you at the beginning about his weak mouth," said her friend Louise, "Never trust a man with a weak mouth."

She'd said the same about Clinton just after he was elected, when everyone else still thought he was wonderful. She should have listened to her.

"You should have listened to me."

"Maybe I've got the wrong end of the stick."

"Yeah, and maybe that's not a wig the Queen's wearing."

Louise knew all the stories they daren't print in the newspapers. But Zoe had seen a side of Gareth that Louise hadn't. In the early days he'd rung her at work to tell her how much he loved her; bought her little presents; written her poems (she'd found them embarassing, and couldn't help noticing some spelling mistakes, but still). At the time she'd thought the sex had been great too, but now, in retrospect, she wasn't so sure. It was hard to tell, she hadn't had many previous lovers to compare him to.

Brendan

Brynley (Oh god, Brynley!)

J. J.

Graham

That boy at Sue's party, after she'd drunk half a bottle of Martini.

That was it.

But all that — the phone calls, presents, poetry, possibly great sex, had stopped. Why? She couldn't help feeling it must really be her fault. If she had been more attentive and spotted the signs earlier, been more understanding, more exciting, more tender, more... something, then it would never have happened.

All this raced round and round in her head till she thought it would burst. It was a relief to go into work, where there wasn't time to dwell on her problems. She was assistant manager at The Happy Carrot Bistro and Healthfood Shop. That morning, like every Thursday, she was carefully preparing the free samples — tempting titbits of pâté, cheese or vegebangers, daintily displayed on crackers. It hadn't boosted sales, it was tedious and time consuming, but she couldn't stop now, the pensioners relied on it. Every week about a dozen turned up. Slowly, methodically, they'd munch their way through whatever was on offer, complaining about the state of the pavements to each other. When they'd finished, they'd say, "Very nice love, see you next week." Off they'd go, for a cuppa in

Littlewood's, before moving on to catch the OAP's Half Price Hour at The Codfather. Anne, the manager of The Happy Carrot, would have had a fit if she'd witnessed such waste. But as she spent nearly all her time in the bistro at the back, discussing soap operas with the regulars, Zoe decided that what she didn't know wouldn't hurt her.

The Happy Carrot was in dire financial straits. The concept of healthy eating hadn't caught on in these parts. *The Argus* had recently run a story about how a local school had halved its truancy rate by offering a Big Mac, fries and milk shake to children who attended classes every day for three months.

Zoe pressed too hard as she was spreading the aubergine pâté, breaking one of the crackers into pieces, slicing into her finger. She rushed to the little kitchen at the back of the shop, held her finger under the tap, cursing herself for being so careless. She stared at the deep red gash. Why had she used such a sharp knife?

Only last week Louise had said, "You're punishing yourself when you should be punishing him."

She stuck a plaster on her finger, rushed back to the front of the shop. The pensioners had arrived and were in a state of excitement, gathered round Mr Williams, who was holding up one of the crackers as if it was exhibit A at a murder trial.

"There's blood on this one."

It would have to be *him* who picked it up.

"It's not blood it's, ah, beetroot juice, one of the bottles must have leaked."

He gave her a withering look.

"I've been in two world wars, I think I know blood when I see it."

She became flustered. The phone rang.

"I'll get it," she shouted at Sharon, who sat at the till, staring into the middle distance with her mouth open.

"Good morning, The Happy Carrot Bistro and Healthfood Shop, Zoe speaking, can you help me?"

"Actually, I was hoping you'd be able to help me."

After work, Zoe walked to the bus station with Sharon, where she caught her bus to Bettws. If the bus wasn't in, she usually stood chatting with her till it came, convinced that she wasn't fit to be left on her own. If The Happy Carrot closed down, she dreaded to think what might happen to Sharon. Or her, for that matter, though Louise had promised she'd get her a job working with her in the Employment Intelligence Unit.

"We visit businesses, spot trends, collect data, write reports saying the working patterns in the province are undergoing an exciting transformation. Do you know that factory wages in South Wales are lower than South Korea?"

Zoe didn't.

"Can you do spreadsheets?"

Zoe pulled a face.

"If they ask you, say yes. Don't worry, I'll be on the interview panel."

"But I *can't* do spreadsheets."

"Zoe, everybody lies these days."

"How's Gareth?" Sharon asked as they walked past the Chartist mural, where a bleary-eyed busker was performing the worst version of *A Design for Life* that either of them had ever heard.

"Fine," she replied, stooping to drop a coin into his filthy hat.

"He hasn't been into the shop for a while now, has he?"

When Zoe didn't answer, Sharon laughed and nudged her, "Isn't he allowed out anymore then?"

"There's your bus," said Zoe, squeezing Sharon's hand. "If you hurry you'll catch it, see you tomorrow."

"No that's the Ringland bus," Sharon replied, but Zoe was already on her way.

She walked into John Frost Square, feeling guilty about leaving Sharon like that. A smiling stranger might be talking her into taking a suitcase full of drugs to Thailand right now. She fought down the impulse to turn back and check if she was alright.

"Zoe!"

She looked up, startled, but couldn't see anyone she knew.

"Over here. To your right, on the bench."

"Josh!"

He smiled weakly. Josh was one of the regulars at The Happy Carrot, drifting through the aisles several times a week like a leaf blown in by the wind. She joined him on the bench.

"I'm sorry, I must be blind."

He shook his head, embarrassed.

"No, it's my fault, I can make people not notice me. The only problem is, sometimes, once I'm doing it, it's hard to switch back."

"Hmmm."

"Last summer I wanted to visit the Outer Hebrides. I didn't have any money but I got the train anyway. The conductor asked everyone for their ticket except me."

"Really?"

"The journey takes hours. I couldn't read a book or anything, in order for it to work I have to keep completely still and stare straight ahead. The effort was exhausting, when I got off the train I had to lie down on a bench for an hour to recover."

"Did you like it up there?" she asked brightly, worried that he was going to dwell on the negative aspects of it.

"Yeah, I got a lot of painting done. All that sea and sky."

Josh was a student at the Art College. She'd tried to persuade Anne to hire him to paint an eye-catching design for The Happy Carrot's window. But she'd taken one look at him and said, "No, it'll be too weird."

"Are you on your way home?"

"Yeah, I'd better get going, actually."

But she made no move. They sat together in silence. Normally, unless she was with Louise, if there was a lengthy gap in a conversation, she'd begin to panic. But now, sitting there with Josh, watching people come and go, she felt strangely calm. After a while, the people passing seemed completely oblivious to their presence.

Zoe flung her book to the floor. It was hopeless, she'd read the same sentence five, six times without it sinking in. Another night eating her dinner alone in front of the telly, another night reading a book. She got up from the sofa, went into the hall, rang Louise, got her answerphone. Of course, tonight was her hot date with Lester. He and his band had just been interviewed by the NME, under the headline *Look Out Manics, Move Over Catatonia, Here Come Tonypandy Five O.*

Underneath there was a photo of him, arms folded across his big chest, legs apart, cocky stare. To Zoe, he looked like a rugby player who'd wandered into the wrong hairdressers'.

"I like a big, solid man," said Louise.

Zoe read one of his highlighted quotes.

We're aiming for world domination. Nothing's going to stand in our way. Being Welsh isn't an excuse for failure anymore.

"Isn't it a bit over the top, they've only released one single."

Louise rolled her eyes.

Zoe, everybody lies these days.

"But he sounds so bigheaded, oh Louise, do you really think it could last with someone like that?"

Louise looked at her as if she was an idiot.

"Who wants it to last?"

Zoe blushed.

"We at the Employment Intelligence Unit think Welsh rock music could be an important source of revenue." She paused, smirking, "And totty."

Zoe was amazed. Louise did whatever she wanted and nothing bad ever happened to her. How did she manage it? She was overcome with anxiety just waiting for her number to be called at the deli counter in Sainsburys.

There was some wine left in the fridge, she poured herself a glass. She drained it in a couple of gulps, refilled the glass, carried the bottle through to the living room, and switched on the telly. She used to be nervous about drinking on her own, but lately had begun to enjoy it. By her third glass, she'd started shouting at Michael Buerke.

"Oh shut up you pompous fart."

and

"We don't care, we don't want to know about the bloody Euro, Buerkey."

She felt reckless and opinionated. She was having a good time!

The phone rang.

"What now?" she yelled, swaying slightly when she got up from the sofa, though she hadn't been interrupted once all evening.

"Yes?"

"Is Gareth there?"

A male voice, vaguely familiar.

"No he's not."

"Ah, he's probably at Dinah's, don't worry, I'll ring him there."

Zoe heard a sharp intake of breath as the caller realised what he'd said.

"Um... I..."

She slammed the phone down.

Jesus Christ!

She marched back to the kitchen, opened a bottle of red.

Leaning against the sink, she stared at a photo of one of Josh's paintings she'd bluetacked to the fridge door. Called *Waiting*, it was a landscape, actually Spurn Point, where he'd grown up, a narrow spit of sand and shingle dangling into the Humber estuary like a shrivelled limb. Nothing was clearly defined, everything was in flux, blending in a Turneresque vortex. At the student show, Josh's paintings were introduced by a notice that read: *Joshua Wainwright's work is inspired by the Irish philosopher Berkeley, who argued that things only exist when attention is payed to them.*

No one payed her any attention, ha! perhaps she didn't exist?

She drained her glass, went to put it on the worktop behind her, missed, jumped back as it smashed on the floor.

"Oh Christ Zoe, get a grip will you?"

She grabbed the dustpan and brush, started sweeping up the broken glass.

"Shit!"

She was in her bare feet, had cut her foot. She flung the brush into a corner in a rage.

You're punishing yourself when you should be punishing him.

She'd had enough, she wasn't going to put up with this anymore. Carefully stepping around the broken glass, she bent over, opened the knife drawer, armed herself, ran out of the door, down the road to Dinah's house. She crouched behind Dinah's overgrown hedge. Gareth was just a few feet away, cheating on her. They never thought about how she might be feeling. Never crossed their minds that she might actually do something about it. Just wait till he came out, he was in for a nasty surprise.

The pain in her foot made her cringe, she shifted her weight, trying to find relief. Something moved just to her right. She jumped backwards. A battered tomcat burst through the hedge. "Jesus!" she hissed, sending it scurrying across the road. She placed her hand on her pounding heart, looked down. Just then the man from No. 29 came round the corner with his collie.

"Are you alright?"

Zoe looked up at him.

"It's a potato peeler. I was going to stab him with a potato peeler."

She held it up, burst out laughing. He took a step back. She noticed a couple in a car parked across the road staring at her, a woman in the house next door to Dinah's peering at her through a gap in her curtains. All thinking *She's gone mad. Lost it completely. Probably dangerous.*

Well maybe I am crazy, she thought.

Relief flooded through her, making her light-headed. She could do anything. She got to her feet, walked through the gate and knocked on Dinah's door. When she opened it, saw Zoe on her doorstep, clutching a potato peeler, her mouth fell open.

"I want to speak to Gareth. Now!"

Dinah retreated slowly backwards down the hallway.

"I feel like the Rhondda," thought Zoe, "Devastated but defiant."

Gareth appeared. He looked bewildered, ashamed, in need of help from a trained counsellor, frankly. Suddenly crazy thoughts began to dance into her head.

He's only doing it to make you jealous. He thought you didn't love him anymore. It was a test, he's been worried sick you'd never notice and he'd be stuck with her for ever. He just wants you to forgive him, then you can start afresh.

"Zoe... you look terrible, why don't you..."

Never trust a man with a weak mouth.

"Come round and collect your things tomorrow while I'm at work. Put your key through the letterbox when you're finished."

"Zoe, don't..."

She turned away after, or possibly before he spoke, she couldn't remember. She walked past the man from No. 29 and his dog, the couple in the car, the woman peering through the curtains, in little over a minute was back in the empty flat.

SAFE

It's a warm, still evening, the last of my leave. Tomorrow I rejoin my regiment, the Welsh Guards. I'm sitting under a horse chestnut tree in Spytty Park, a bottle of whisky in my hand, a baseball bat at my feet, waiting. From here I can keep an eye on the Carmarthen Street entrance, the playground, across to the pond, down to the bandstand. Nothing can get past me.

I'm a professional.

I joined up eighteen months ago. I probably should have thought more carefully about what I wanted to do when school ended. Or thought at all. I just hoped something would turn up. Nothing turned up but a YTS scheme, dragging tyres and shopping trolleys out of the canal.

After I'd been on the dole for four years, I began to lose it. One night I dreamt I was digging my own grave in the garden. When I'd finished, I lay down in the hole, and began covering myself with earth. Someone started calling my name, I ignored him, I just wanted to be left alone. But the bastard wouldn't give up, he kept on shouting, until eventually I woke up. It took three mugs of sweet tea and half a packet of chocolate biscuits to get rid of the taste of dirt in my mouth. That's when I decided something had to change.

I arrived at the Army Recruitment office too early, they hadn't opened. There was a cafe just a few doors down, but I wouldn't allow myself to go in.

There's no rush, I'll go home and sleep on it, see how I feel tomorrow.

No. No. No.

I stayed where I was, looking at the photos in the front window.

Join the Professionals.

Nothing about Northern Ireland. Maybe it wasn't compulsory, perhaps there was a box on the form — *Please tick here if you do not wish to be sent to Northern Ireland.*

I was still grinning at the idea when the sergeant came to open up.

"Something funny?"

I shook my head. He looked a right hard bastard, I didn't want to get on the wrong side of him. I followed him inside, sat down. "So, why do you want to join the army?"

"I want to do something useful with my life."

"Is that right?"

The hint of a smile appeared at the corner of his mouth. For a moment I thought he was going to lean back in his chair and say "Who are you kidding sonny?" He came from the same sort of place as me, somewhere at the end of a branch line where the trains don't stop anymore, somewhere uneconomic, where the weeds were sprouting and the junk was piling up.

Cwmhopeless
Llangrotty
Benefit Mountain
Girotown

Somewhere you didn't say "I want to do something useful with my life" if you knew what was good for you.

All the same, I nearly walked out. It was only three days to my next giro, a few quid in my pocket, a few beers inside me, I'd be alright again. But I didn't, I stayed where I was, and signed on the dotted line.

I take a swig of whisky, light another fag. There's a screech of tyres as a car takes the corner of Carmarthen Street, Queen blaring on the stereo:

WE WILL, WE WILL ROCK YOU.

Bass nearly taking the roof off, tatooed arm beating time on the door. A bottle flies through the air and smashes on the tarmac, glass tumbles down the path. From the car a drunken cry of "Fucking hell!" as it roars away down the road to some other dead town. After a few beers they'll be singing "Hello, hello, we are the Ponty boys" at the top of their voices, till the locals steam in to defend their patch. Another Saturday night in the Valleys.

That's all there is to do around here, drink and fight.

Sometimes you only have to walk into a pub in another

town, or the wrong side of your *own* town, to get your head kicked in. My kid brother, Richie, had his nose broken in a chip shop in Mountain Ash. He'd dyed his hair green, worn a tee shirt with Oscar Wilde's face on it, *I Have Nothing To Declare But My Genius* written underneath. I warned him not to go to Mountain Ash looking like that.

My mother never goes out at night anymore. There are four locks on our front door, she keeps all the windows shut tight even in the middle of summer, there's a poker under the bed ready to beat off the robbers, rapists and lunatics.

You aren't safe anywhere these days, terrible it is.

I couldn't sleep again last night. Eventually I got up, I knew there was a half bottle of whisky in my jacket pocket down-stairs in the hall. As I put my foot on the top step, there was a loud creak.

"Is that you Richie?"

"No mam, it's me, Mark."

A long pause; the only sounds my dad's heavy breathing next to her in the bed, the hum of the fridge downstairs; my heartbeat.

My heartbeat.

"What are you doing?"

"I can't sleep, I'm going to get a drink."

Another pause.

"Put the light on, you could fall on those stairs in the dark."

I heard her turn over in the bed. I thought I heard a stifled sob, but I might have imagined it. I went downstairs, and sat drinking whisky at the kitchen table till the numbness returned.

Ever since I can remember, everybody round here has felt defeated. You can smell it in the air, see it in people's faces, read it in the graffiti on the underpass.

SINCE I GAVE UP HOPE I FEEL MUCH BETTER.

Or the scrawl over the poster for the Job Club.

DRUGS NOT JOBS.

The crap houses, the crummy shops covered in wire mesh, the smashed up phoneboxes, the wrecked cars — after a while you start to think maybe we don't deserve any better, it's our fault, we're no good.

I'm sick of feeling numb. I'm going to fight back.

The government has spent thousands of pounds transforming me from just another pleb into a lean, mean fighting machine.

Germany was great. I'd never been abroad before. I loved everything about it. The beautiful forests where we trained, the old town squares, the mad drivers on the autobahns, the Bierkellers, the Frankfurters and Sauerkraut.

The Fräuleins.

I loved the way they seemed to have everything under control, sorted out, in order. Every single German was confident, strong, intelligent. Every last one of them looked like they expected life to be good to them, and it was. The towns weren't dirty or run down, people hadn't given up. Yes, Germany was great.

Then they told us we were being sent to Northern Ireland.We spent three days preparing for the tour in Tin City, a "village" in the middle of the English countryside. It looks just like any real village — houses with milk on the doorsteps, shops, pubs, a graveyard on the outskirts (a nice touch that). You go on patrol, stop a civilian, ask his name (the population, you can't help noticing, is 95% male). When he says "Mr Patrick O'Sullivan, of 19 Monaghan Road", you ignore his cockney accent, his squaddie haircut, the West Ham tattoo on his arm. You're dying to say "Come off it mate, who do you think you're kidding?" or "This is stupid, do we really have to do this?" But you daren't, the cameras are recording everything, a special team of advisors are monitoring your every move. So, you radio for a computer check; they tell you the information's correct. You thank Mr O'Sullivan, walk on, scanning the windows, corners, doorways, for snipers. You are a professional.

We'd go out on patrol in Tin City the first couple of times, nothing would happen. Mr O'Sullivan, Mr Flaherty, or Mr Fitzpatrick would co-operate, no problem. Then, the third time, gun shots would come from one of the windows, a bomb would explode, petrol bombs flew through the air. They had you jumping out of your skin.

Then there were the riots.We must have had nine or ten in those three days. Blokes from the Royal Anglian hurling bricks, yelling "Up the IRA" and "Go home you Brit bastards."

At the end of it, we were convinced it was going to be like bloody *Apocalypse Now*.

The night before we left, they briefed us on all the different organisations — the IRA, INLA, UDA, UVF, though I don't know how much good it did, given the average squaddie's attention span.

Gerry Adams? Isn't that the bloke who invented Thunderbirds?

Of course I had an advantage over the others, you see I'd already been briefed by Richie, before I left. Richie never had a job in his life, never been further than Bristol, but he had an unshakeable opinion on every subject under the sun.

"It's like this. Over there, the Protestants are the English, the Catholics are the Welsh, end of story."

"That's just fucking stupid, that is."

"No man, I'll tell you what's stupid, you going over there to keep the Welsh in their place."

Professor Richie Evans, Chair in International Relations, University of Ponty.

He was always a bolshie bastard, the amount of times I had to wade in to stop him getting his head kicked in. But he didn't mean half the things he said, he was only trying to get a reaction, he'd say anything to try and keep the boredom at bay.

I pick up a handful of stones, begin chucking them at the swings where Richie and I used to play when we were kids. I can see us now, as if it was yesterday, talking about what we were going to do when we grew up.

"Stunt man," I told him.

He pulled a face.

"Too dangerous."

We'd watched a documentary about stuntmen a few days before. One guy broke his neck when he didn't fall the right way.

"What about you?"

"I'm going to get a job in one of those booths at the end of the Severn Bridge, collecting money from people who want to visit Wales."

"You spaz, you don't get to keep the money, you have to hand it over at the end of the day."

"No you don't."

"Yes you do."

Anything that wasn't too much effort, that was Richie.

He was two years younger than me and we always hung around together. Gary, my older brother, was a bastard, but I always took care of Richie while I was here. If anyone touched him they had me to answer to.

"Leave him alone."

"He called me a moron."

"He didn't mean it."

"I did."

"Hey!"

"He didn't. Now fuck off."

Peace keeper, that's me.

When I came back from Germany on leave me and Richie went to Newport for the day. We had a pint, then went to the Art Gallery in John Frost Square, to see an exhibition by students from the art college. I knew that would get him going. Richie was brilliant at art. His teacher wanted him to apply to art college. But he wouldn't listen, he was going through his Che Guevara phase at the time, planning to head for Nicaragua straight after school, and fight for the Sandinistas.

He was soon foaming at the mouth.

"Christ, if that was mine, I'd have hidden it under the floorboards."

"Jesus! Rolf Harris could have done better."

"Thinks he's Jackson Pollock, more like pretentious bollocks."

And so on, till the attendant came rushing over.

"Excuse me, can you keep your noise down."

That was the cue for Richie to start waving his hands at the paintings, shouting at the top of his voice in a terrible French accent:"Zis is an outrage. Zis is not art, zis is, ow you say? Doggies' doo doos."

"Out! Now!"

We ran down the stairs, laughing, went for a drink in The Murenger.

"You're a better artist than any of those."

"Tell me something I don't know."

"So what's stopping you?"

"Eh?"

"Why don't you get off your arse, get a dossier together."

He started laughing.

"Portfolio."

"What?"

"It's called a portfolio you pleb, not a dossier."

"Whatever. Get one together, apply to the art college here in Newport."

"Yeah... I might do that."

"Might? Come on Richie, it's time you did something with your life."

"What, like you?"

Though I didn't need any, I got up and bought another packet of fags from the machine to stop myself from smacking him one.

Took my time unwrapping the cellophane and lighting up, letting him sit there, stewing. When I came back he was staring at the floor, ripping a beermat to shreds. As I sat down he whispered something.

"What was that?"

"Sorry."

"So you fucking should be."

He knocked back the rest of his pint in one.

"Fancy another?"

I grabbed his arm.

"No, we haven't time. You're going to take me to an art shop, and I'm going to buy you whatever you need — brushes, paints, paper, whatever."

"I don't want your money."

That was a laugh. I'd paid his fare, bought his fags and drinks; earlier in the week I'd given him a tenner so he could see a band in Pontypridd, a fiver to get a mate's birthday present. At least that's what he said.

"You can pay me back later."

He laughed.

"How?"

I hated seeing that expression on his face — *Come on, you know I'll always be broke.*

"I'll tell you how. By getting into art college. Unless you're afraid to try."

I could see the hurt in his eyes. But I knew the kind of rut he was stuck in, knew how difficult it was to break out of. Get wrecked for a couple of days after his giro came, then go out of his mind with boredom for the next two weeks.

The first time I saw Belfast, I felt cheated. It was so fucking normal. Just like Cardiff, or Swansea. Sometimes you had to remind yourself you were in a war zone as you walked past W.H. Smiths and Spar, past women pulling shopping trolleys, past men coming out of the newsagents' carrying *The Sun* or *The Daily Mirror*. The people look like us, speak the same language, watch the same tv programmes, support the same football teams. Some of them are the enemy, most of them aren't. It does your head in.

When we first arrived, the continuity NCO from the previous tour walked around the district with us, pointing out all the hoods. He had P cards for all of them, with their name, address, age, what they'd been arrested for, all kinds of personal details.

We were glad of that information the first time we patrolled the Divis Flats. What a dump, built in the Fifties, but already falling apart. The rubbish chutes were always blocked, crap was piled up everywhere. Soldiers had broken all the lights in the passageways between floors to make it harder for snipers, so at night it was pitch dark. You'd hear the rats scrabbling along the corridors.

I'd heard so many stories about that place. I didn't believe most of them — but still, they left an impression. Being hit by used nappies or tampaxes flung from the balconies; savaged by an alsatian in one of the corridors; opening the lift and finding a dead baby in a bag on the floor. The RUC never went there without the army to cover them. For two blokes from the RUC to patrol in bulletproof jackets you'd need twenty soldiers on the ground, another eight in land rovers, a helicopter, and the Quick Reaction Force on standby. All that, just so they can say *Look, see the coppers on the beat? Everything's normal.*

The first time we walked into the Divis, I was terrified.

Suddenly I was sure all those stories were true.

It was Mike and Lewis's first tour as well. The corporal, Iestyn, had been there before, he knew how to keep his nerves hidden. He led the way, eyes taking in everything, like a hunter. The flats were full of snotty-nosed, shrieking kids and their foul-mouthed, chain smoking-mothers.

"Look at the wee boy with the great big gun."

"Couldn't you get a proper job then sonny?"

"Bet you wish you'd tried harder in school now, don't you?"

"Thatcher's fucking tin soldiers."

Iestyn smiled at them and said, "I suppose a shag's out of the question then, is it?"

That cheered us up.

"Fuck off you dirty Brit bastard."

Iestyn winked at them.

"More! More! I love it when you talk dirty to me."

We walked on, big grins on our faces.

Then he saw what he wanted — one of the hoods who'd been pointed out to us. A tall, scrawny, fair-haired young guy.

Leaning against the wall of the bookies, one hand in the pocket of his jeans, the other holding a fag. Head back, surveying his manor. He smirked when he saw us, took a long drag on his fag, and blew out a couple of perfect smoke rings. Iestyn smiled back, walked straight up to him.

"Hello Christy, how's it going?"

It was brilliant. The guy was gobsmacked, wondering how the hell this soldier he'd never seen in his life knew his name. Iestyn stepped a little closer.

"Don't forget to send your brother Aidan a birthday card next week, will you? Stuck in The Maze for the next twenty years. He must need cheering up."

It was the lad's worst nightmare come true — the Brits knew everything about him. He tried to look cool, but it was no good, he'd lost it, we could see it in his eyes. We were pissing ourselves.

Hello, hello, we are the Ponty boys.

There's a pub on the estate, that's where we went next. It stank of stale cigarettes, beer, meat pies and sweat. A few old guys were playing cards in one corner. There was a gang of six or seven young bucks sitting round a table to our right. The barman looked like a wrestler gone to seed, the kind of bloke who kept a baseball bat under the counter. On the wall behind the bar, postcards from the States, a Dodgers pennant, a poster of Bobby Sands smiling, an Irish tricolour. Everyone stopped talking, the only noise was the sound of *The Men Behind the Wire* on the jukebox. We made straight for the gang of lads. You could tell they'd been sitting there for hours. Their eyes were slow, bleary. The ashtray was overflowing with butts, the beer-mats were in shreds, peanuts were mashed into the pools of stout. It must have been giro day. Iestyn picked out the biggest one, sitting right in the middle.

"Hello there Kevin. Are these the ones you were telling us about?"

You could see Kevin wanted the ground to open up and swallow him. The whole pub was staring at him. I don't know how long it took him to convince his mates he'd never seen us in his life before, or whether he got a kicking before they eventually believed him. But the main thing was, we planted a seed of doubt in their minds. We rattled the bastards. Showed them we weren't going to be messed about.

We were on a high when we got back to the barracks that night.

Lewis was telling anyone who'd listen "We did the Divis today — piece of cake." Which was a real joke, because he'd have crapped himself without Iestyn to hold his hand. But I realised then what I liked about the army. It puts you right up against what you're most frightened of, so that you have to confront it. In civvy street you've got the option of avoiding anything too scary, and you're always going to take that option, let's face it. But in the army.

That was Richie's problem, for all his smart talk he was frightened, he just couldn't face up to things as they really were; he lived in a dreamworld. The things that boy was going to do.

"I'm going to hitch around South America."

He bought a second-hand Spanish phrase book, lost it after a week.

"I'm going to start a band."

He learnt two chords on the guitar, cut his finger, retired.

"I'm going to join the PLO."

He got as far as sticking a photo of Yasser Arafat on his wall.

"I'm going to be a beach bum in the South of France."

He couldn't find any swimming trunks that suited him.

But Richie could always make me laugh. Once a tourist coach pulled up alongside us in the town centre. The driver rolled down his window and shouted at Richie and me, "Can you tell me the way to the Black Mountains?" The passengers were looking round anxiously, wondering what they were doing in this dump, where was all the beautiful scenery they'd been told about. Richie banged on the window, shouting "This is Ponty. The doors are locked, do not get off." The coach driver swore under his breath and pulled away.

Then there were the answers he wrote on that stupid form you have to fill in when you sign on.

What job are you looking for?

Artist.

What other jobs would you consider?

African game warden, marine biologist, rock star, helping Bob Geldof, commander of ship to sink all whaling fleets, playing the lead in the new James Bond film, carrying David Attenborough's suitcase, astronaut, collecting the toll on the Severn bridge.

What do you plan to do next to find work?

Buy a magnifying glass with my first giro and look for it.

Could you start work today?

No.

Why not?

Because half the day's gone already.

They suspended his benefit.

He ended up on a YTS scheme, cleaning up the next stretch of the canal from the one I'd cleared a couple of years before.

It was Richie who answered the phone the first time I rang from Belfast.

"Hi-ya Rich, how's the portfolio going?"

"OK."

"Have you applied to art col?"

There was a long pause before he muttered, "Not yet."

"You'd better get your act together. If you're not careful you'll be too late to get in *next* year, let alone this."

"Stop giving me such a hard time, will you?"

"You think I'm giving you a hard time? Try doing my job. Try marching through the middle of Belfast in broad daylight, never knowing when a sniper might take a crack at you, or if the next car you pass will explode, hey!"

He dropped the phone, it clattered on the table.

"Richie! Richie!"

I was shouting for quite a while before my mother picked it up.

"Mark?"

"Richie put the phone down on me. Tell him to come back here now, I want a word with him."

"He just went out."

"What's the matter with him?"

"Mark, he's driving me mad. He's been like this ever since he got that letter from the art college a few weeks ago."

"He actually applied?"

"Yes, but they turned him down. They said he needed to work more on his — oh I don't know, those words they use. But they suggested he try again next year, they obviously thought he was good."

"Shit, I thought he'd get in."

"He just mopes around the house all day now. I can't get a word out of him. No wonder he's got no energy, he doesn't seem interested in food anymore. Well that's no good, is it? If we all chucked in the towel like that after the first setback..."

"Yes mam."

I had a feeling there was something else going on, but I couldn't put my finger on it. Anyhow didn't I have enough problems of my own? What was I, a fucking social worker?

I've been sitting too long, I have to stretch my legs. I get up, walk over to the swings. I stand up on the swing, using my arms and legs to push it higher, till I'm horizontal at the top of the arc. The air roars in my ears, the trees blur into a green smudge at the edge of my vision. Action Man.

"Yeee-es!"

I'm laughing like a madman.

"I'm a professional!"

Something's moving to my right, between the bandstand and the pond. Fuck. I jump from the swing, land awkwardly scrabbling on all fours. Then I'm up and running, reaching the tree in a couple of seconds, I grab the bat, roll over and lie flat in the grass. I'm ready for them.

It's a dog. A scruffy black mongrel. He jumps over the fence and starts drinking from the pond. It's a full minute before the owner appears, an old guy, painfully struggling up the hill, leaning heavily on his walking stick.

False alarm.

That was slack. I musn't get sloppy, must keep my concentration. Come on Mark, wake up. Don't blow it. My heart's thumping like a jackhammer. I let go of the bat, return to my hiding place and take another drink.

When I was a kid, this place would have been full of people on a fine summer's evening like this. Not now though. There are some pretty unsavoury characters hanging round the park these days. The police don't seem to care.

I care.

I joined the professionals but I never did get to jump from a plane, or give the thumbs up from a tank. Everyone tells you Northern Ireland is the Big One, you're no one in the army unless you've done at least one tour. Well we spent four solid months walking up and down the same streets in Belfast, day in, day out, and nothing ever happened. No bombs, no riots, no shoot outs with the IRA or the UDA. It was almost as boring as Ponty. When I was bored I wished I was terrified, when I was terrified I wished I was bored.

Being stuck with the same bunch of blokes for so long is no picnic, after a while little things about them drive you mad. The way Mike never stops sniffing; Iestyn's cough; worst of all, Lewis's moaning, the bastard never stopped.

"This food's bloody rubbish."

"This beer's bloody piss."

"My feet are bloody killing me."

"I never get any bloody post."

Right I thought, you want some post do you? I started cutting out the Freepost adverts from the papers, and filled in the coupons in his name. He got bullworkers on seven days' free trial, incontinence pants, books on positive thinking, a Learn Chinese in Three Months casette. On our last day there he received an apology — *Dear Private Williams, we regret that because of the present troubles in Northern Ireland we are unable to send you a conservatory on seven days free trial.*

Iestyn told us how it used to be.

"I was here in '69. We didn't have a bloody clue what was going on."

We were sitting in the barracks one night, having a drink; we were allowed two pints of beer a day over there.

"The first time we faced a riot, the captain shouted 'This is an illegal gathering. Go home now, or we'll open fire.' A complete waste of time, he couldn't make himself heard. So he orders a couple of us to unfurl the banner with the official warning written on it. The rioters took one look at it and fell about laughing. It was written in Arabic, we'd been in Aden the week before."

I don't know what the hell we were doing there really. A bunch of blokes from Wales, patrolling the streets of Belfast while everything was falling apart back home. I started to dread ringing our house. Then one day my mother burst into tears when I asked her about Richie.

"Oh Mark, we had to ask him to leave."

"Why?"

"He was stealing all the time. He stole from my purse, he stole my jewellery — he couldn't have got much for that, God knows. He stole your dad's rugby trophies, your bike — he was selling anything he could get his hands on."

"How long's this been going on? Why didn't you tell me before?"

"We didn't want you worrying."

"How do you think I feel now?"

"Don't take it out on me. I've tried everything to get through to him. It's no use. I couldn't cope anymore. We've had all the neighbours banging on the door, accusing him of stealing from *them*."

"Where's he gone?"

"A squat on the other side of town, over in Rhyderin."

"Couldn't dad have tried to sort him out?"

"Don't make me laugh."

He spent every night down the working men's club where no one has a job, getting pissed, reliving the glory days of Welsh rugby.

I saw the English players literally trembling when they came out of that tunnel and onto the pitch at the Arms Park.

Big deal.

"You two were always close, maybe he'll listen to you when you get home."

I couldn't understand how it had got so bad so quickly.

Yes I could.

The last few jobs disappearing, cheap smack flooding the streets. After a few weeks in West Belfast, I was suspicious of every kid I saw on crutches. The IRA kneecapped drug pushers. They knew that once that stuff got into the kids' systems they were good for nothing. Too numb to hate the Brits.

This is Ponty. The doors are locked, do not get off.

Captain Phillipson knew why we were there, he didn't have any doubts.

"It's up to the politicians to come up with a political solution. Our job is to protect the RUC."

We walked around the Shankhill, watched them hanging union jacks over the streets, taping photos of the Queen to their windows. Phillipson said "Sad, isn't it? You'd never see this kind of pride in being British back home."

Sometimes you'd turn down a street, see the mountains at the end of it, and for a moment you couldn't believe you weren't back home. At least they've got the murals over there to provide a bit of colour. Some of them are brilliant. Green hills sweeping down to a bright blue sea; Celtic heroes riding into a blazing sunset; portraits of Nelson Mandela and Bob Marley. Some turn your stomach; a phoenix rising from the ashes, provos coming out of the flames, firing guns and mortars; a dying hunger striker, looking like Jesus Christ; a stick of dynamite, the fuse burning, under Britain.

If Richie had got into art college, you never know, he might have got somewhere. It could have been the first step on a glittering international career.

A painting by the young Welsh artist Richie Evans today sold at Sothebys for a million pounds.

Another phone call, just a week before we finished our tour of duty. My mother's voice trembling as she spoke.

"A gang of blokes wearing balaclavas broke into Richie's squat, smashed the place up, and beat up him and the other boys. They warned them to leave or they'd be back."

She blew her nose, tried to collect herself before continuing.

"They painted *Kill All Junkies* on the front door."

"Has he got anywhere else to go?"

"He's heard about another squat... I'll bet it's a pigsty."

"I'll be home soon. We'll get him help."

"Mark, he looks terrible. Where's it going to end? I don't

want to lose another son."

Gary had disappeared before a court appearance and had never been seen again. I had a third brother, John, he chased a ball into the road and was run over by a van when he was six.

You're not safe anywhere these days.

"You be careful out there, Mark."

"Don't worry about me mam, I know how to take care of myself."

Iestyn told me that the the number of casualties the army pick up in Northern Ireland in twelve months are about the same as the number of soldiers killed each year in road accidents. The army had taken good care of me; I was well trained; had the best equipment; back up was only minutes away.

But who took care of Richie?

I wasted four months in Northern Ireland, when I could have been back here, doing something useful, like keeping my brother out of trouble. But I learnt something over there in Belfast, I learnt something from the Irish. It's not defeat you smell over there in the streets, it's fighting spirit.

It was Iestyn who gave me the idea.

"The police are bloody useless. They should send us in, we'd soon sort them out. Don't tell me local people don't know who the dealers are. One platoon would take care of them."

It was Captain Phillipson who told me. It was our last day in Northern Ireland. We were getting ready to go out on the piss, congratulating ourselves on getting through it without so much as a scratch when Iestyn walked in, said Phillipson wanted to see me. His face, his voice, told me something was up.

I finished buttoning up my shirt, followed him down the corridor. Iestyn knocked on Phillipson's door.

"Come in."

That plummy voice of his. All the officers are English.

"Yes corporal."

"Private Evans to see you sir."

"Ah..."

A pause, papers being shuffled, the sound of a drawer being closed.

"Show him in, corporal."

Phillipson sat behind his desk in his white shirt, his black bow tie, still untied, dangling from his collar. A pair of gold cufflinks on the desk in front of him. A cigar started, then hurriedly stubbed out in the ashtray, the smell still lingering.

Behind him on the wall, a photo of the Queen.

I knew before he said anything. It was obvious from his expression that this was something he'd been dreading having to do since he'd become an officer.

"I'm afraid I've some bad news, Evans."

I found myself staring at his Adam's apple rising and falling as he spoke. I'd never noticed how large it was before. Suddenly I couldn't take my eyes off it. He made a steeple with his fingers, looked down at it, frowning.

"There's no easy way to put this."

He pursed his lips, looked up, trying to fix me with his eyes. I stared at the Queen, her eyes were as blank and cold as a fish on a slab.

"Your brother, Richard, is dead."

Even though I knew what was coming, when I actually heard him say it for a moment I thought my legs were going to give way. I gritted my teeth, I took a deep breath, closed my eyes. When I opened them again, he was staring at me anxiously. I realised he was worried I'd lose it, and he'd have to deal with it.

"I'm dreadfully sorry. It must be a terrible blow."

"Sir."

It had to happen. It was only a matter of time. If he'd got that place in art college in Newport, he would have been alright.

They're all speed freaks down in Newport, smack's never really taken hold there like it has in the Valleys, where kids have fuck all to do. Now I realise he was already on it that day we went there. That money I gave him earlier in the week, there was no band, there was no friend's birthday, I paid for his fix.

I wonder if Phillipson knew how he died?

I hear he was a drug addict. What a tragic waste of young life. Something needs to be done about that kind of thing. It's up to the politicians to come up with a political solution.

He ran his hand through his hair.

"I know how you must feel. I've a younger brother myself.

I'd be mortified if anything happened to him."

But nothing will. They don't have a drug problem in Cheltenham. He frowned, "Normally we would grant emotional leave for a matter like this, but as we're all going home tomorrow anyhow..."

"Yes sir."

Richie was dead, and no one would pay, no arrests would be made, no one would be blamed but himself. The cops don't care, why should they be bothered about a nobody like Richie?

It's easier for the Irish, they know who to hate. The Brits are to blame for everything.

Richie would have been safer in Belfast. The Provos would have kneecapped him when they found out he was a smackhead. Better to end up on crutches than lying dead on the floor in a dirty squat.

Somebody's coming.

It's him. At last! Strolling slowly towards the crumbling bandstand. He sits down, starts rolling a fag. I pick up the bat, skirt slowly round the back way. By the time I'm behind the bandstand, two nervous-looking kids are walking towards him, anxious for their fix. He looks up, they exchange nods.

I'm in place, almost close enough to reach out and touch the back of his head with the bat from here. The two smackheads can go, I'm not interested in them. It's him I want. Him, and all the others like him who poisoned Richie and got off scot free. Now he's going to pay. I take the balaclava from my pocket, pull it over my head.

Gary's gone; John's dead; Richie's been murdered.

I'm the last of the Evanses.

The numbness has disappeared. I feel alive. I'm angry. I don't care what happens to me, the important thing is that someone is finally fighting back.

With one hand I tighten my grip on the baseball bat, I lay the other on the edge of the bandstand, ready to push myself up.

I'm a lean, mean, fighting machine.

Here I come.

OFFA'S DYKE

My father was forced to flee the country in order to avoid conscription and became an exile in Peckham. Even then he couldn't afford to relax. Leaning over me as we walked down the street, he'd whisper, "The National Coal Board often send their top agents over the border to track down Welshmen who've escaped the mines. If anyone starts asking questions, we're up on a day trip from Swansea see, and can they tell us the way to Madame Tussaud's please?"

I nodded, right you are dad. The English led such boring lives, but even a trip to the corner shop was an adventure for us.

We weren't the only exiles. There was an Irish family living next door. They had a boy my age called Kieran. When I stood on top of the never to be finished model of Caernarfon Castle I was able to rest my arms on the garden wall and start a conversation.

"Is your dad on the run too?"

He stared at me, then turned and walked into the house without uttering a word. I'd never met anyone so shy.

No hiding behind false beards or dark glasses for my father, he concealed his true identity by getting a job as a bus conductor. What a stroke of genius that was, parading up and down in front of the English, taking their money off them, as bold as brass. The conductor was the most important person on the bus. Any twit could drive, but it took fantastic skill to keep public order, remember all those fares, and keep your balance on the platform as the bus hurtled round corners.

The driver had to wait for *his* orders. He pulled a cord when he wanted him to stop, and rapped on the side with half a crown when he wanted him to go again. I loved it when he did that, it was just like a member of the resistance giving one of their secret signals in a film.

Knock Knock. Who's there? The Welsh Resistance! I've got a gun and I'm not afraid to use it. Take this bus to Cardiff.

When I told them I was Welsh in school it only provoked them. There were fights. I learnt how to look dignified in defeat and act aloof as they shouted "Go back home Taffy."

My father put his arm around my shoulder, gently shaking his head.

"Go home indeed. They don't know what they're talking about. We were here long before them. When the Romans invaded Britain it was ruled by Celts. The Anglo Saxons, that mob the English are descended from, didn't even arrive till the Romans left. We were here first, why don't they go back to Germany?"

So they were Germans. It explained everything. The Germans in my comics were always arrogant bullies, taking over other people's countries and strutting round them as if they were the rightful owners.

"History is written by the powerful, and in their version the small countries don't get a look in. You'll only get one side of the story in school, but any time you're not sure of something the teachers or the other children have told you, come and ask me. You promise?"

"I promise."

"Good boy. Us Celts have to stick together."

Shortly after that, he changed his route to one that went right past the school. As soon as the last class was over I would run outside and wait for his bus to arrive. On the journey home, he would sing songs, tell stories, or pull funny faces behind stuck up passengers. People would ask if he was my father. When I told them he was, they'd smile and say "That's nice!"

Although we lived in exile, we said blow the risk and went

back home every year for our summer holidays. Sheltering under a bus stop from the downpour, my father explained that you needed the rain to keep the country green and gorgeous.

"Can you imagine Whatshisname writing a book called *How Brown Is My Valley*?"

If the rain didn't bother him, I wasn't going to let it bother me. I slowly stretched my neck out like the tortoise on *Zoo Time* till I could see the Welsh flag patch that my mother had sewn onto my anorak. My father had bought it for me the day before, it was the first time I'd worn it.

"We've some of the best scenery in Europe here in Wales. I walked the length of the Pembrokeshire coastal path one summer. Glorious. Another time I hitched a ride to the Elan Valley just so I could see a red kite. You daren't touch them, they're a protected species, protected by the Gurkhas actually, and I was up those Brecon Beacons every chance I got."

My mother crossed her arms and started talking to the roof.

"And rushed back to the breathtakingly beautiful streets of Port Talbot in time for your tea, you were a right little Billy Whizz, weren't you?"

He gave her a funny look, then carried on.

"They're so unfriendly in England, I miss the fantastic community spirit we had when we were growing up."

"Everyone's nose in your business."

"No one ever locked their doors. No need. I never met anyone who'd been robbed till I came to London."

My mother made a noise just like a horse snorting.

Back in the bed and breakfast he'd be full of high hopes for tomorrow, when it would have rained itself out. We'd hear him singing *Ying Tong Diddle I Po* in the bath. He loved funny songs, he knew *Right Said Fred, Little White Bull, My Old Man's a Dustman* and *Donald Where's Your Troosers* all off by heart. When he came out of the bathroom, hair all Desperate Dan after a vigorous towelling, shiny pink in his white vest, he'd laugh and say no wonder the country was full of reservoirs.

Muhammad Ali was fighting Henry Cooper. The English hated

Ali, loved Our 'Enry. My father was the only man in work supporting Ali. He was the latest in a long line of black Americans that he admired, joining Sugar Ray Robinson, Sidney Poitier, Martin Luther King and Paul Robeson. He had a big stack of Paul Robeson records, and his wonderful voice often filled the front room on Sunday mornings. Kieran came round with his enormous dad to watch it on our telly. Mr Ahern filled up the room like a film star, Burt Lancaster or John Wayne. The chair disappeared under him and his booming voice bounced off the walls.

"That Cooper is an ignorant pig. Fancy refusing to call the man by his proper name."

He mimicked a cockney accent.

"He'll always be Cassius Clay as far as I'm concerned."

He banged his fist on the arm of the chair.

"What business is it of his what he calls himself?"

"Aye, the English have never liked people having foreign sounding names. They always try and change them. Look what they did to us. Their law courts saddled us with Anglicised versions of our names and insulting nicknames because they couldn't be bothered to pronounce them properly. There's an old rhyme about it;

Take ten, he said, and name them Rice,
Take another ten, and name them Price,
Now Roberts name a hundred score,
And Williams name a legion more,
And call, he moaned in languid tones,
Call the other thousands — Jones.

So you see Cooper's just carrying on the ancient English tradition of sneering at other people's cultures. He'll be taught a lesson tonight though."

Mr Ahern turned and fixed me with a grave stare.

"Your father is a scholarly man, you listen to what he says."

Then he turned back to him.

"They did a good job on us too, spent hundreds of years trying to stamp out our culture and language. We've got a lot in common, sure what is a Welshman but an Irishman who can't swim."

They started telling each other what great qualities the Welsh and Irish shared, while Kieran and I arm-wrestled to decide who got the last Wagon Wheel. My mother made us stop and broke it in half, then she went into the front room with a glass of whisky and her jigsaw of The Great Wall of China. She didn't like boxing and Mr Ahern gave her a headache; she reckoned they could hear him back home in Cork.

When Cooper knocked Ali down there was a blood-curdling cry from Mr Ahern, then a terrible silence filled the room slowly, like water rising to the ceiling. Kieran and I looked at each other, disbelieving. Dad brought in more beer and pop and told us it wasn't over yet, but he looked worried. Ali hung on and recovered. When he got his strength back he beat Cooper till blood streamed down his face, shouting:

"What's my name? What's my name?"

Cooper wouldn't say his proper name, so he got beaten even worse. The room went cold and my stomach started churning, I was glad when the referee stopped it.

Afterwards my father and Mr Ahern were all smiles, touching each other on the arms and pointing.

"Drink up Frank, you're looking at a rich man. I had bets on Ali to win with half the bloody garage."

"What will you do with your winnings?" asked Mr Ahern.

"I think I'll buy a knighthood. I'll be known as Lord Edwards of Port Talbot."

Mr Ahern laughed, Kieran laughed, I looked at them all lit up from inside, and I started laughing myself.

The next day the school was full of moping English, whose fathers had told them that Our 'Enry was going to teach that big mouth a lesson. I bobbed and weaved along the corridor chanting "What's my name? What's my name?"

"Taffy," shouted Smirky Perkins.

We were on the Pwllheli train. All you could see were caravans, thousands of them, each one the same, stretching along the coast in single file. When I looked at my father he smiled and nodded at them.

"That's where we keep the English."

A huge crowd of people got on at Aberdovey, struggling with bursting suitcases, pushchairs that refused to fold up and squalling, sticky children. My father surveyed the chaos, lowered his *Daily Mirror* and whispered ominously "Brummies!"

Since the train was nearly full already, most of them had to stand. They stretched right down the carriage, gripping seat corners, squashed against each other. Before long they were ooohing and aaahing as they twisted their heads to see the dramatic mountain scenery on one side and the sea on the other.

As an old Welsh lady struggled to squeeze through and get off at Llwyngwril she lost her temper.

"Roll on winter, I can't stand these crowds."

My father turned to me and said, "God created Birmingham as a warning to us all."

My mother dug him in the ribs with her elbow.

"Sssh, someone will hear you."

He lowered his voice.

"It must be terrible to grow up in a cultural desert, trapped in a tower block, surrounded by ring roads and motorways. No history, no tradition, how could you live not knowing where you really came from?"

"What do *you* know about it?" asked my mother angrily. "How would you feel if an Englishman saw a crowd of poor Welsh people making a bit of noise sightseeing in the middle of London and started saying how uncultured they were?"

He waved a hand dismissively.

"Not the same at all."

My mother sighed and shook her head, which seemed to cheer him up. A superior smile appeared on his lips and he returned to studying the Brummies.

Some Saturdays Kieran and I would travel around London on the bus with my father, sitting on the long seat by the door, swinging our legs and swapping sticky sweets, watching the performance. "Any more fares now please? No? Any requests then? Welsh favourites, light opera, music hall, pop?"

The passengers would glance at each other sheepishly.

"*Men of Harlech*!" Kieran shouted.

"Right you are, Master Ahern, *Men of Harlech* it is."

And he'd stand by the stairs and sing so beautifully. We always led the applause, turning round to the passengers and smiling, encouraging them to enjoy themselves.

He'd wanted to be a singer, had been offered a place in a top music college, but had to go out to work to support the family, since his father had gone off the rails. He'd bitten his tongue and got on with it, until one day he could bear it no longer, and he ran away.

"If only I'd had the proper training, who knows how far I'd have gone. Who knows?"

He'd look into the valley of broken dreams, sad eyed, sighing. I didn't know how to help him.

"You don't need any training, you're a great singer," I'd say.

He'd lean down and hug me, run his hand through my hair.

"And you're a great son."

I didn't know if I was sad even though I was happy, or happy even though I was sad.

They started calling him Tom down the garage. After Tom Jones. "I suppose it makes a change from being called Taffy," he grumbled, fooling no one, you could see how delighted he was.

He'd stand on the edge of the platform in traffic jams, one hand gripping the pole, the other stretched out towards the trapped drivers, singing *The Green Green Grass of Home*. Some of them thought it was *Candid Camera*.

"No it's Tony, finest singer on the number 8 route," he'd shout back, beaming like the Latest Big Thing.

As part of my education, he took me to the cinema to see *Zulu*. He was delighted that a neglected piece of glorious Welsh military history had been made into a film. The Zulus overran all the English regiments, but met their match when they attacked a company of South Wales Borderers, even though they outnumbered them a hundred to one. Stanley Baker was their leader. My father said he was a fine actor about a thousand times, till eventually a man sitting behind us shushed him.

The Zulus charged, beating their spears against their shields and singing their war songs, *the same songs that had struck terror into the English.* When Stanley saw how nervous his men were, he turned to them and shouted "Sing". Then he stared straight back at the thousands of advancing Zulu warriors and started singing *Men of Harlech.* But his men just stood there, gawping. Stanley was furious when he realised he was singing on his own. He shouted "Sing! Sing, damn you, sing!" at them. They finally remembered who they were, and started singing *Men of Harlech* at the top of their voices.

The Zulus stopped in their tracks, they'd never seen anything like it in their lives. Now both sides faced each other singing. No matter how loudly the Zulus sang, and how fiercely they beat their spears against their shields, the South Wales Borderers sang back, heads held high, thrusting their rifles at them. *Come on,* they seemed to be saying, *come on down here if you think you can beat us. But before you do, there's one thing you should know. We're different from that last lot you slaughtered. They were English. We are Welsh. Don't say you haven't been warned!*

They fought the Zulus to a standstill. At the end of the film, just when Stanley's men had nearly run out of ammo, and could barely keep their eyes open, the Zulus appeared once more at the top of the hill overlooking the fort. They stood there, chanting.

"Why don't they attack? What are they up to now?" asked the men. "Why are they taunting us like this?"

One of the old African hands started laughing.

"They're not taunting you, you fools. They're saluting you as brave warriors."

Then the Zulus shook their spears one last time, turned and left. Stanley walked away from the others, stood on his own, lay his gun down on the sandbags. He stared out into the darkness, thinking about how close they'd come to defeat, about all the men he'd lost. I saw dad wiping away a tear.

On the way home he became bitter and said that when you thought about it they'd only been fighting for someone else's

Queen and Country. He took me to see it again the next week though.

In the privacy of my bedroom I practised looking as tough as Stanley Baker.

"We stay where we are and fight."

Putting on our plastic macs in The Mumbles ("This is where Marlon Brando learnt to act") my mother and I watched him surge ahead as it started to drizzle, singing "What a glorious fee-eeeling, I'm happy again" in his Neddy Seagoon voice.

She tapped ash off her cigarette, sighed.

"It's all make believe, the whole bloody lot of it. Not a bit of common sense, god help him. Don't dream your life away like him David. Will you?"

I refused to answer. It started to pour down, I heard her sighing again.

At breakfast the landlady smiled at him when she brought the pot of tea.

"I heard you singing this morning, what a lovely voice you've got."

"He sings on his bus in London," I said proudly.

"Ooh, listen to him. He's a right little cockney now, isn't he?"

I tried to unnerve her with my Stanley Baker stare.

"He's Welsh all right. Aren't you son?"

In London I was.

Smirky Perkins sidled up to me in the playground.

"My mum got on your dad's bus the other day. She said he was running around singing and making a fool of himself in front of everyone. When he saw her, the big twit started singing *Delilah*. He's a nutter."

"He was only trying to cheer her up, she's always going about with a long face on her. He tries to cheer all his passengers up. The English don't know how to enjoy themselves, they haven't got any community spirit."

"He's a stupid Welsh twit. You wouldn't find my dad running around singing and making a fool of himself."

"I'll bet he can't sing, I've never seen him smile, no one likes the miserable bugger."

"He's not there to be liked. He's the boss, people have to do what he tells them. The English are born leaders, all the Taffies are good for is singing and yakking."

"Shut your stupid English face."

"Go back to Taffyland you sheepshagger."

He banged my head against the wall. No chance of being thought a cockney here.

"Don't mention the investiture to your father," my mother warned, as soon as I came in. She tapped her forehead.

"I've had it up to here with it."

A German had been made Prince of Wales.

When my father came home he borrowed an axe from Mr Ahern and smashed up the never to be finished model of Caernarfon Castle, then made a bonfire out of it.

That day bombs were planted across Wales.

"Have you heard the news? Two people have blown themselves up," he said bitterly, as we ate dinner.

"Why did they do that?" I asked, making my mother wince.

"Don't be so daft, they didn't do it deliberately. What do you think they were, bloody Kamikaze pilots?"

I felt my face burning. My father pushed his plate away, muttering.

"Give me strength."

He went back into the garden and I looked through the window and saw Mr Ahern hand him a bottle of beer over the wall. He looked furious as he talked to Mr Ahern and swigged from the bottle, shouting about the need for a republic. I heard Mr Ahern shouting.

"Stupid looking big eared eejit."

My mother shook my shoulder.

"Leave them to it. We're going on holiday soon, that'll cheer us all up. Come on, come and help me with my jigsaw of Spaghetti Junction."

Dad took us for a walk along Offa's Dyke towards the end of the holiday. It felt very strange, standing right on the border. On one side was Wales, on the other, just a few feet away, England.

Dad had gone very quiet. I asked him what he was thinking. He started complaining about all the English people living around there. They pushed up the house prices wherever they went, making it difficult for us to move back.

"It's not just that though, what would you do if we did move back, where are the jobs?"

My mother quickened her pace after she'd spoken, wanting us to move on before he got morbid.

"They reckon over a million people have left Wales this century because there's no work for them in their own country. England has always lorded it over us, just taking what it wants and spitting out the pips."

"Come on Tony, let's enjoy ourselves, it's a beautiful day. Life's too short for brooding."

He didn't seem to hear her. He stood there, chewing on a piece of grass, staring at England.

"If only we could have kept them out."

He looked tired and defeated.

"If only."

On the train back to London I stood in the corridor on my own, thinking. I leaned out of the window, as stoney faced as Stanley Baker.

We stay where we are and fight.

On my first day back in school the teacher asked us to talk about what we'd done in the summer. I told the class how we'd gone to the Wye Valley and walked along part of Offa's Dyke. When Smirky pretended to yawn, I raised my voice.

"It was very interesting to visit such an important historical site. The Welsh people built Offa's Dyke to keep the English out of their country."

The teacher, Windy Waller, started laughing.

"I'm afraid you've got it the wrong way round Edwards. It was an English king, Offa of Mercia, who built it to keep the Welsh out of his kingdom."

Everyone was staring at me.

"No, it's you who've got it the wrong way round."

I could see Windy was starting to lose his patience.

"What makes you so sure?"

"My father told me."

"I see, he's a historian is he?"

Smirky shouted, "He's a bus conductor" and everyone burst out laughing. Eventually Windy started banging his duster.

"All right, settle down, settle down."

I sat through the rest of the class in silence, furious and ashamed. As I was leaving school at the end of the afternoon my father's bus pulled up at the stop outside. He was standing at the back, singing *Men of Harlech*. I couldn't bear to see him after what had happened, and hid inside the school gates while he anxiously looked around for me. When he didn't see me, he got off the bus and started walking towards where I was hiding. My heart pounding, I crouched down out of sight and squeezed my eyes shut. I heard his footsteps getting closer and closer. Then they stopped, he turned around and walked away again. I held my breath till I heard the ding ding of the bell and the bus driving away.

BACK THEN, WE THOUGHT THE CLASH WERE GOING TO CHANGE THE WORLD

"Hello Janice."

"She's in her room."

Janice retreats to the kitchen. A strong smell of fresh coffee, the radio on low, tuned into Jazz FM. I knock on Debbie's door.

"It's dad."

The door flies open, Debbie pushes past, struggling into her leather jacket, whispering urgently "Let's go, go, go!" We go. But as soon as we're out of the front door, she curses under her breath, turns round, and flies back inside.

"Well?"

"Well what?"

"Aren't you going to tell me not to go out looking like this, not to drink, smoke..."

"Do what you want."

"You're pathetic!"

The lift arrives just as Debbie storms out of the flat again, slamming the door behind her.

Before starting the van, I say "I thought maybe we could go up to Hampstead Heath, since it's such a nice day."

Debbie shrugs.

"Is there something else you'd like to do instead?"

She places a strand of hair in the corner of her mouth, begins chewing it.

"OK, here's the plan — go for a walk on the Heath, get something to eat, then see a movie. How's that sound?"

"Whatever."

It's Sunday morning, half past nine, the roads are clear. I roll the window down, feel the fresh, strong breeze blowing against my cheek. It feels good to be on the move, leaving all our problems behind, just like the characters in a road movie.

"What do you get if you play country music backwards?"

Debbie stares out of the window, gnawing her little finger.

"You sober up, your wife comes home, and your dog comes back to life."

Stony silence.

"What film do you fancy seeing?"

"Don't care."

"There's a *Time Out* down there if you want to check what's on."

No reaction.

"There's an Aki Kaurismäki double bill at The Everyman this afternoon. *Hamlet Goes Business* and *Leningrad Cowboys*. You like his stuff. Remember *I Hired a Contract Killer*? You loved that one."

"Uhhnnn."

This was supposed to be my ace. She thought *I Hired a Contract Killer*, about a lonely man who hires a hit man to put him out of his misery, only to fall in love while he's waiting to be taken out, was the best thing she'd ever seen. I was delighted, I'm a huge fan of Aki's, and had a feeling that she'd dig him too. Afterwards, she wanted to see every film he'd ever made. That was last month.

"I brought you the latest copy of *Message in a Bottle*."

She mumbles, "Thanks."

This is the poetry magazine that I help produce and write for in my spare time. I've included a couple of my new poems. I'm particularly pleased with one of them, *Flicks*, which chronicles the different stages of my life through my visits to the cinema. My mother taking me and my brother to see *The Incredible Journey*; feverish adolescent groping in the back seat during *Maid for Pleasure*; watching *It's a Wonderful Life* alone on Christmas Eve, after splitting up with Janice; Debbie and I crying at the end of *Cinema Paradiso*. There's no sign of interest from Debbie about this either.

"Things a bit heavy with your mum right now, huh?"

She moves her head ever so slightly in my direction, treating me to her most scornful expression.

We sit in silence for a few minutes, then I dig out my tape of the first Clash album, put it on and crank the volume right up.

*

I park the van in the free car park near the ponds. The Heath looks trampled to death, scorched, parched. The prospect of walking across it with Debbie fills me with self pity. All it would have taken was a quick phone call, saying the van wouldn't start or I had a stomach bug, and I could have been snuggled up in bed with Sasha right now.

My head begins to throb, I'm still dehydrated after last night, too much Budvar.

"I fancy a cold drink, how about you?"

She shrugs.

I walk over to the shops to buy the drinks, while she sits in the van, her chin propped in her hand.

I hold the ice cold can to my forehead as we trudge up towards Parliament Hill, kicking up dust clouds, the cool droplets from the can mingling with salty sweat. My leather jacket is slung over my shoulder, Debbie doggedly continues wearing hers, though her face is bright red by now. She only bought it a few weeks ago, in Camden Lock, after months of nagging me for a contribution. When I finally coughed up, then offered to go with her, she froze in horror.

I'm still getting the silent treatment from Debbie. I choose the steepest path to prove I'm not getting old; to burn off some of my frustration; to try and force a couple of words out of my darling daughter, even if they are "Fuck you." When we reach the top, she collapses onto the nearest bench, gasping. I take care to look bitterly disappointed, as if I'd have loved to keep going for another hour or two, before finally sitting down next to her. It's a clear sunny day, no pollution haze, you can see for miles across London, from the Post Office Tower to Canary Wharf. Debbie sips from her can. I open mine, drink half of it in one go, take out my tobacco tin and begin rolling a fag.

"Do you want one?"

"Yeah."

I hand her the first one I roll, pass her the lighter, then take out another paper.

"You don't seem in a very good mood, Debbie. Want to talk about it?"

"Uh oh, is this meant to be, like, quality time with my dad."

She starts knocking the lighter on the arm of the bench.

"You don't have to talk about anything if you don't want to. We can just sit here."

"That'll be fun."

She scowls, delicately extracts a stray strand of tobacco from her lips.

"Look Debbie, I love you, you know? But right now you're doing my head in. I'm probably having the same effect on you. And if you don't want to spend time with me, then just say so. I'll drop you off wherever you want to go, and you can do your own thing. No one's forcing you to stay."

Her face falls.

The first of the kite fliers walks past, clutching a bright red rhomboid. I finish rolling, close the tin, put it back in my pocket.

"Can I have my lighter?"

She drops it into my outstretched hand with a show of great reluctance, then takes a long drag from her roll up.

"You'd rather be spending the day with Sasha, wouldn't you?"

It's my turn to shrug. I light up, then rub the ball of my thumb up and down the roller on the lighter.

"As a matter of fact, Sasha and I aren't getting on that well at the moment."

"That's a shame," she says sarcastically.

"I'm not looking for sympathy. It's hard work living with someone. There's lots of ups and downs."

"Tell me about it."

She starts tapping her ring against the can, making a loud, irritating noise, then says "Perhaps you should go and talk to someone about it."

This is a reference to the time a few weeks ago when I suggested she and her mother go see a counsellor if things were that bad. Rather than trying to drag me into it.

"Yeah, maybe we'll do that," I say, hoping I sound like a calm, unruffled adult who'll gladly add her helpful suggestion to my list of possible solutions. We don't say anything for a while. "Look at that jogger," I say, glad of the distraction, nodding at a middle-aged, bare-chested, very overweight man. He's hobbling along at snail's pace below us, wearing a walkman, a grubby white poodle trotting along beside him.

"Ugh, he's gross!"

"He's either very brave, or very stupid, I can't decide which."

"It's incredible, it never seems to occur to men that their bodies might be disgusting."

I wonder if she's quoting Janice? Surely she couldn't have come up with that on her own at her age?

"I wonder what he's listening to," I say, ignoring her assault on the male sex. Debbie tries to blow a smoke ring, fails, screws up her face in annoyance. The red kite soars up into the sky.

"You used to like kites, remember?"

"No I didn't!"

You'd think I'd accused her of clubbing baby seals. I'm well aware that I was the one who was really keen. I'd always wanted a kite when I was a kid, but my parents wouldn't get me one. When Debbie was five or six, I bought her a beautiful Spiderman kite from a shop in Covent Garden. The trouble was, she lost heart so easily. If the wind wasn't very strong, and it was hard to get the kite going, or too strong, so that it was difficult to control, she'd start to whine and demand to be taken home. Janice refused to come with us, she thought kites were for morons.

"What is there to do here, anyway?"

As if she didn't know. She'd been here dozens of times with me. Enjoyed herself. But today, she's determined not to have a good time. That would be giving in.

"Walk, talk, look around, chill out."

"I'm bored."

"I'm not. I like it here. It's a nice place to be."

"What's the point of coming somewhere nice, when you have to go back to the same old dump a few hours later? It's not worth it, it only makes where you live seem even worse."

"Forget about a few hours from now. Live in the present. You might feel better."

"Huh!" she replies scornfully, making me feel like one of those trendy vicars on *Thought for the Day*, trying to sell some cliché as a great insight. I'm determined not to show my irritation.

Suddenly I stand up, lob my empty can into the bin, pick up my jacket.

"Come on."

"Why?"

"Because."

After about a hundred yards I stop, pretending to notice something on the horizon, giving her the chance to catch up with me.

"I need the lighter again," she says, irritably.

I hand it over, noticing a blue kite in the sky to our right. I look down to see a father with his son, laughing with joy as they watch it soar and swoop in the breeze. Debbie returns the lighter, we carry on.

"How far to the next bench?"

I groan, flick my butt into the air.

"You know Debbie, sometimes things that don't seem that great at the time can seem really special when you look back later."

She laughs derisively, "You mean, like, this?"

"Yep, that's exactly what I mean."

"So, tell me, what will I find so special about today when I look back on it."

"Well, the day's hardly begun but, you never know, at some point we might actually get on with each other. That'd be something."

She squints at me suspiciously.

"That's what I'm hoping anyway," I say, giving her an ironic smile, swiftly walking on before she can think of a sarcastic answer.

Debbie and I approach Kenwood, locked in sullen silence. Another year or two, she'll move out, no matter what Janice says, and that'll be that.

Debbie, your dad's on the phone.

Oh god, tell him I'm out.

I notice a pregnant woman and her young son staring up at an oak tree. There's a plastic football stuck in one of the lower branches.

"Oh Jamie! Why did you have to kick it so hard?"

Jamie is on the verge of launching himself into an almighty tantrum. Just what I needed, an opportunity to help someone, make me feel good about myself.

"Is that your ball up there?"

Jamie stares at me, open mouthed.

I wink at the woman.

"We'll soon get it back."

"Please, don't put yourself to any trouble."

"It's no trouble."

I toss my jacket on the ground, rub my hands together, then begin clambering up the trunk. When I reach the branch where the ball's stuck, I turn round and smile at Debbie, standing a couple of paces behind Jamie and his mother, her face a mixture of anxiety and embarrassment. I carefully edge out onto the branch, knock the ball down with my hand.

"There you go."

Jamie runs after it, yelling. His mother crosses her arms over her protruding belly, saying "Please be careful."

I smile winningly. Just as I'm preparing to jump the last few feet, I lose my grip and fall, landing awkwardly on my ankle, then pitch forward onto the ground, hitting my head on a large stone.

"Oh my god!"

"Dad! Dad?"

"Jesus, fuck!"

I lay still, my hands over my face, groaning, footsteps running towards me. When I take my hands away from my face, a lean, fit looking middle-aged man with bulging eyes forces his way between Debbie and the mother. He gently touches my chest with his fingertips.

"Whatever you do, don't move."

"My ankle, I think it's broken."

"Marge, Marge!" he bellows over his shoulder, making Debbie and the mother wince. "I need your bag."

Marge hurries over, clutching a canvas bag. He takes it off her, raises my head, places the bag underneath it. Despite the pain, I feel like an absolute pratt. Debbie looks lost, I want to shout out "Somebody take care of my daughter!" More people begin to gather. The man starts to speak very loudly and slowly, as if addressing a foreigner with little English.

"How many fingers do you see?"

And

"I don't think you're concussed, but you should report to

the hospital, you can never be too careful where the head's concerned."

Then

"Can you move your ankle?"

I can. He touches it very gently with his fingers.

"Aaagh! Jesus Christ! It's completely buggered."

"I can assure you," he laughs pityingly, "if your ankle was broken, there's no way I could have put that much pressure on it without you screaming your head off."

I have to get away from this man.

He places the flat of his hand firmly on my chest.

"Not so fast."

I wave him away.

"I'm alright."

He removes his hand, backs off slightly.

"You should take a few minutes to recover. You've had a very nasty shock."

I try getting up, but the shooting pain in my ankle stops me. I curse under my breath. His hands flutter around my shoulders, ready to push me back down.

"What did I just tell you?"

"Get out of my fucking face!"

"Charming..." mutters Marge. The man's gaze turns cold. Someone behind me starts giggling.

I struggle to my feet, supported by Debbie, who looks on the verge of tears.

"Don't worry, I'll be alright," I tell her, taking her hand. When we're safely out of earshot of the crowd she says, "That was *so* embarrassing."

We reach the cafe at Kenwood, I collapse into the nearest chair and hand Debbie my wallet. She returns from inside with a pot of tea, apple juice, cakes. I pass her one of the roll ups I made while she was away. We eat and drink in silence for a while. A hideous lump is beginning to form on my forehead. My ankle's killing me. I reach inside the pocket of my leather jacket, bring out the copy of *Message in a Bottle*, hand it to her.

"You're in the one on page 23."

Despite herself, she looks interested, then suspicious. While she's reading, she pushes a lock of her hair behind her ear, and smiles.

"So you *did* cry in *Cinema Paradiso*."

"Yeah."

"You tried to pretend you didn't. I don't know why, everyone else in the audience was crying their eyes out, why should you be any different?"

I raise my eyebrows.

"Do you like it?"

"Yeah, it's really good. You know, you should organise some more readings, that one in The Rosemary Branch was great."

"Yeah, it went OK."

"Come on, it was more than OK. I'll bet you sold twice as many magazines that night than you usually do in months. Didn't you?"

"Probably."

"So you should organise another one, right?"

I hold up my hands.

"OK, OK! Yes, you're right. I will."

She looks pleased with herself.

"So, have *you* written any poems lately?"

She shakes her head dismissively, as if only an idiot would ask that.

"You don't think they're any good."

She screws up her eyes at me.

"I'd like to see them."

"What for?"

"Maybe I could help. I've read so many poems that people were convinced were no good, and all they needed was some editing."

This is a lie.

"No way."

"Debbie, I keep telling you, you're good."

"For my age."

"Don't be so hard on yourself."

She slides down in her plastic chair, stares at the ground. The subject is closed.

"You know what I think?" I say.

"About what?"

"That bloke who rushed over to help — he roams the Heath every day, looking for people to 'help.' He's obviously a psycho. God knows what was in that canvas bag his wife was carrying."

She rolls her eyes, "I thought there was going to be a fight." She takes another drag, then nibbles at her little finger.

"Good job it happened up here, eh? Where none of your friends could see you."

"I haven't got any friends."

Before I could stop myself I say "Debbie, I wish I knew how to make you happy."

She jerks her head away, as if someone had just forced something unsavoury in front of her.

"You know what I think?" she replies, still looking the other way. "You have to be stupid in order to be happy. If you have any idea of what's going on around you in the world, there's no way you can enjoy yourself."

"You can't feel responsible for everything, Debbie. That's crazy."

"You're right, I probably am crazy." She prods the sides of her head with her index fingers, "Nothing that 20,000 volts won't cure."

She rolls her eyes, bares her teeth.

"Debbie..."

She resumes her normal expression.

"What about you? Are you happy?"

"Sometimes."

"How often?"

"I don't know. Not as often as the Waltons, but more than Morrisey, OK?"

"What about when you were my age, were you happy then?"

It sounds like she's testing out her latest theory, that unhappiness is in her genes. This is her research.

"No, I wasn't very happy. My parents were always fighting. Me and my brothers were always fighting. Everyone was fighting. The only way you could avoid getting your head kicked in was to join a gang. It was funny, you'd see all these blokes swaggering around in gangs, pretending they were great mates, but you knew half of them hated each other's guts. It was just insurance."

"Did you join a gang?"

"Nah! I was never one for gangs."

"So you got your head kicked in a lot?"

"Yeah, loads of times," I tap my head. "I reckon I got brain damage. That's why I never made anything of myself, ended up delivering organic vegetables."

I start laughing, it turns into a coughing fit.

"So, come on, was there ever a time when you were really happy?"

I pause, take a long drag from my roll up.

"Yeah, during punk. It was brilliant. For the first time I was in the middle of something really important. It felt like the thing I'd been waiting for all my life. There must only have been about a hundred punks in the whole of London when it started. It felt really great whenever you saw another punk on the street, it was great to know you weren't on your own, after hours of being stared at as if you were a freak."

She smiles wearily, she's heard it all before.

"You know what you're saying?"

"What?"

"The only time you were ever really happy was when you were in a gang."

"Nah!"

She shakes her head.

"It's true."

"Nah!"

"Nah!" she shouts back, imitating me perfectly. She brushes some ash from her leg.

"Punk didn't last long though, did it?"

"No. We thought The Clash were going to change the world, but it didn't happen."

With my good foot, I crush an empty can that's rolled under the table. I could kill a pint, I wonder how long it would take me to hobble over to The Spaniards?

She knocks her ring slowly against her bottle of apple juice three times, as if deciding something, then takes a swig.

"You know what really drives me mad about mum?"

She looks at me sideways, wondering how I'd respond to her breaking my no bitching about Janice rule. When I don't say anything, she continues.

"The way she's always telling me how lucky I am. How

happy I should be."

I suppress a smile. This is a bit rich coming from Janice.

"Why should you be so happy?"

"Because I'm sixteen. If she was sixteen again she'd be delirious. I'm supposed to be this big failure because I'm not walking round with a stupid grin on my face all the time."

I don't know where this is leading, but it feels important not to lose it.

"There's nothing so great about being a teenager. If you want my opinion, it's the worst time of your life. I'll tell you something that I've never told anyone else before, even your mum."

She slowly arches an eyebrow, as if auditioning for the part of a Bond villain, leans back in her plastic chair, waiting.

"When I was eighteen, me and this mate of my mine, Wilf, were coming back from seeing some punk band in South London one night, when two massive skinheads started following us. Wilf had a red mohican, big pair of boots, a skull and crossbones on the back of his leather jacket, but the bloke couldn't knock the skin off a rice pudding. Me, when it comes to skinheads, my fighting technique consists of curling into a ball and hoping they'll give up. It's about half eleven at night, there's no one else on the streets. Every time we look behind us, these two evil looking skins are getting closer, staring right at us. We head for the British Rail station, I'm praying that a train will be leaving the station as we arrive, so that we can jump onto it like The Professionals and escape in the nick of time."

Debbie laughs at the thought of me and Wilf attempting a Bodie and Doyle.

"We get there, the station's empty. No sign of a train, not another soul to be seen anywhere."

I stub my fag out in the saucer, blow the smoke out of the side of my mouth, Debbie's has gone out but she hasn't noticed.

"I look behind me. They're still coming. 'Right,' I say to Wilf, 'We'll split up. You stay on this platform, I'll cross over the bridge onto the other one, that might throw them.' When I'm half way across the bridge, I look behind and see both of them following me. I am crapping myself. I walk along the platform, trying to look cool, all the time the sound of these two pairs of size ten Doc Martens getting closer and closer. I reach the end of the platform. There's nowhere else to go. Before I know it they're standing either side of me. I'm the meat in the sandwich. The sweat is pouring off me. They bring their heads right next to mine. They're so close I can hear their watches tick, smell their hot, foul skinhead breath. Still I daren't look round, I keep staring straight ahead, too terrified to meet their eyes. Suddenly both of them shout 'BOO!'"

Debbie jumps.

"Then they walk off, laughing."

We weigh each other up for a moment, then she gets the giggles.

"OH — MY — GOD!"

Her eyes squeeze shut, her shoulders shake, she covers her mouth. When she opens her eyes again, I lean closer, lower my voice.

"I wanted to crawl into a corner and die."

I hold my index finger and thumb a centimetre apart.

"I felt about this big."

She bites her lip, embarrassed, uncertain how she should react.

"But you know what?"

"What?"

"I got over it."

Suddenly her expression hardens.

"*I'll* get over it too, right? This *phase* I'm going through."

She adopts her complacent, smarmy adult voice.

"I don't know what's come over Debbie, she used to be such a *nice* little girl."

"Let's not get carried away."

She narrows her eyes.

"Debbie, why do you have to twist everything I say?"

"I don't. It's you, you never say the right thing," she replies, sitting up.

"Let's face it, if *I* said it it wouldn't be right, would it?"

We're shouting now, the people at the other tables are staring. I stare back.

"We're having an argument — big deal!"

Debbie groans.

"Well done. Oh God, why is it always *us*?"

"I don't know. I don't know much I guess. It's a bummer, isn't it? You want a cool, totally sussed dad, I want a happy, confident daughter."

I shrug.

"But we're stuck with each other. What do you think of that?"

She doesn't reply, doesn't need to, the panic in her eyes says it all.

A WITNESS

Keith walked up the long, steep road from the seafront to the railway station, whistling *A Pair of Brown Eyes*. It had been a good day; he had some great material. Now he was looking forward to grabbing a window seat, a coffee, shaping his article in the comforting motion of the train. Then, as he passed the registry office, a door flew open, a man came racing down the steps towards him.

"Please — can you help me?"

An East European accent, late thirties to early forties, tall, good looking, dressed in a white linen suit, a blue carnation in his buttonhole.

"I'm waiting to get married. We need two witnesses, but we only have one. Can you spare a few minutes?"

Keith checked his watch, it was twenty to three. There was a train back to London in ten minutes, it was over an hour till the next one. The man gripped his arm.

"It really won't take long."

"I'm not exactly dressed for a wedding," replied Keith. The man looked him up and down. He was wearing trainers, an old pair of jeans, a tee shirt, the words *Drink! Girls! Feck! Arse!* in lurid green beneath Father Jack's scowling face.

The man shrugged.

"Father Ted, yes? Everyone loves Father Ted. Please, this way."

Keith smiled. Why not? It might even make a good article.

The bridegroom held out his hand as they walked up the steps.

"My name is Miroslav."

Keith shook it.

"Keith."

He followed Miroslav into the registry office, down a high, wood panelled corridor, lit by a cheap chandelier.

"None of our guests have turned up. I don't know what's happened to everyone. This is a nightmare. An absolute nightmare. It's here," he nodded at a door on the left.

In the corner, a clerk scribbled in a huge ledger. A painting of a newly married Victorian couple hung over the mantelpiece; dried flowers filled the fireplace. The registrar stood in the centre of the room, irritably brushing dandruff from the shoulder of her black jacket. Two people sat in front of her. Another East European man, and Rachel.

Miroslav said, "I've found someone."

Rachel turned, saw Keith staring at her.

"Perfect."

"You know each other?" Miroslav asked anxiously.

Rachel rolled her eyes.

The registrar looked pointedly at the clock, "I'm marrying another couple at three. So unless you have any objection to this person being a witness, I think we should start."

Miroslav turned to Rachel.

She groaned; "If it's OK with him, it's OK with me."

Everyone turned to Keith.

They met in a cinema, stumbling into each other in the dark, racing for the exit an hour into *The Draughtsman's Contract*.

"Sorry."

"Sorry."

As soon as they realised they were both headed for the pub opposite, they burst out laughing. Keith held the door open for her as they entered.

"I definitely need a drink after that."

There was an empty table in the corner.

Rachel took a drag from her cigarette, sipped her pint of lager.

"They wouldn't fall for that kind of nonsense up north. They'd surround the box office and demand their money back."

"It wouldn't get shown in South Wales, it's against the law there to show any film that doesn't have Charles Bronson in it."

They discovered they were both in their final year, Rachel at UCL, Keith at RADA — "I'm the token oik." Before long he was telling her about the play he was writing, the one he was certain would make his name; she didn't look bored or seem to think him ridiculous, so he continued.

An hour later, the friend Rachel had left behind in the cinema came into the pub looking for her, as arranged. By then it was crowded, smoky, the juke box was booming; the friend looked uncomfortable as she strained to spot Rachel, who waved, but didn't stand up.

"She *still* can't see me. She must be blind. Oh well, I'll give her a ring tomorrow."

She disentangled herself from Keith, rolled over onto her front, checked the time on the radio alarm.

"2.25. Oh god, we're going to be popular."

She cringed.

"These walls are so thin, we probably woke the whole block up. Things are a bit tense round here."

Her finals were a week away.

"Do you wish you'd spent the night revising?"

"No, a girl's gotta have some fun."

He leaned over, brushed her hair to one side, kissed her neck. They lay together for a while, not saying anything, listening to each other's breathing in the dark.

"What are you thinking?" he asked eventually.

"I was wondering if this is a flash in the pan, or the real thing."

"It's too early to say."

He started to laugh.

"Ssssh! What's so funny?"

"I just realised I was quoting Mao Tse Tung. That's what he replied when someone asked him what he thought of the French revolution."

"Hey! Don't you dare write your play when you're in bed with me."

Down the corridor a door opened, closed; they fell silent as someone walked past, on their way to the bathroom.

Rachel turned over to face him.

"My problem is I expect too much, too quickly, when I start having a relationship with someone. Then I get very hurt and angry when it doesn't work out."

He ran his fingers gently down her cheek.

"It won't be like that this time."

She grabbed his wrist; her grip was much stronger than he expected.

"Can I trust you?"

"Yes," he replied, alarmed at how cracked and dry his voice sounded in the dark.

The four of them sat in a row — the other witness, Miro, Rachel, and Keith, desperately trying to work out what was really happening. Rachel wasn't the marrying kind. He figured she must be doing this so Miroslav could stay in this country. He'd heard the going rate for such arrangements was around £2000, but he was certain she wouldn't have taken any money. But then even if she were marrying him just so he could stay here, it still didn't rule out them having a relationship, did it?

It had been four years since he and Rachel had split up. He'd often wondered what had happened to her. Now he was surprised how numb he felt. It took him a few minutes to realise he wasn't allowing himself to feel anything till he'd found out what was really going on here.

There was a knock on the door. The registrar paused.

"Yes?"

A group of embarassed guests shuffled into the room.

"Um, sorry we're late."

There were three more East Europeans — an elderly couple, and a younger man carrying camera equipment. Then some Brits — a couple of guys, and three women, the one with grey hair accompanied by her daughter.

The registrar waited till they were settled, then said, "Well, if we're all sitting comfortably, I'll carry on."

Keith's play was called *Another Saturday Night in Deadend*. The characters were trapped in a dreary town on the edge of the Valleys, not a million miles from Bridgend, where Keith grew up. The actors often turned away from the rest of the cast and addressed the audience directly, telling them their innermost thoughts. The prop forward was in love with the scrum half, the policeman was a secret transvestite, that kind of thing. Keith, when asked to describe it, called it "My revenge on

Bridgend" or, after a few drinks, "A kind of punk *Under Milk Wood*", pretending it was a joke but secretly hoping someone would agree. Staged in a room above The Artichoke, a seedy pub near The Elephant and Castle, it ran for a week. Audiences were small.

At least he had been able actually to get some acting work out of it, playing Mervyn, the frustrated intellectual, who'd spent years trying to teach his parrot to quote Schopenhauer:

"Life is a sorry affair, and I am determined to spend my life at home, thinking about it."

He'd hoped his performance might attract the attention of an agent, having almost given up hope of getting work through auditions. The last one he'd attended had been particularly traumatic. The advert in *The Stage* said the production was "Seeking new faces for an exciting experimental production." The director sat stony faced while Keith began performing one of Mervyn's interior monologues as his audition speech. He'd hardly spoken more than three or four sentences before he cut in.

"OK, OK, that's enough. Now, walk across the room like a woman."

"Pardon?"

The director stared at him for a few seconds before repeating his instruction.

"Oh, that's what I thought you said."

But after just a few steps, months of anger and humiliation fetched up in Keith's throat, he turned to the director and yelled, "I don't have to do this. *You* walk like a woman!"

"We'll let you know."

The director turned away, started looking down his list for the next name.

"Don't bother," said Keith, picking up his jacket, heading for the door. "I'm going to get a normal job."

They ate in one of those cheap Indian restaurants in Brick Lane where you brought your own booze.

"When I started teaching, I had all the idealism of Tony Benn," said Rachel, breaking off a piece of nan bread, dipping it into her chicken madras. "But after a couple of years working in Tower Hamlets, I seem to have turned into Norman

Tebbit."

She reached for her glass of wine.

"I just want to pack the whole bloody lot of them off to a labour camp."

"I don't know how you can stand it."

At one point, in his desperation to get an equity card, Keith had briefly considered applying for a Theatre in Education job. But, in the end, the thought of working in schools had been too revolting. His parents had expected him to go into teaching, "to put something back into the community", give other working class kids the chances he had. But he wanted nothing to do with the community ever again, had had a gutsful of it in Bridgend.

Rachel knocked back most of her glass in one go.

"I don't want to end up like the others. Burnt out, cynical about everything."

"Then pack it in."

He wanted the old Rachel back. The warm, funny, energetic Rachel.

"That's easy to say, but what am I going to do instead?"

"Anything — just get out."

She frowned, pushed some rice around the plate with her fork. Keith knew she could never drift through temporary jobs like him. He resented the fact that he had to go to work at all, when he could have been at home writing his latest play, or sitting in a cafe, leafing through *The Stage* or the sports section of *The Guardian*. He hadn't had a job for the last six months, it didn't bother him a bit.

Rachel finished her glass, poured another, smiled brightly.

"Never mind, maybe your new play will make you into a household name. We'll buy a house on the coast. I've always wanted to live by the sea."

"On a clifftop, overlooking a secluded bay," said Keith, happy to see her mood improve.

"I'll be a woman of leisure. We'll have two kids. You can stay at home and write, and look after them during the day. I'll get a nice, relaxing job as a gardener, or something to do with conservation."

Keith felt an unpleasant chill run down his back. He liked having the place to himself in the day. Often he wrote listening to pounding rock music. He'd type up a scene, then walk around the room, acting it out, flinging himself around the furniture, shouting at the top of his voice. He knew, from his limited experience, that babies and young children were startled by loud noises and sudden movements. He tried to picture himself having to write silently, never daring to jump from his seat, being interrupted by a screaming toddler with a dangling nappy, demanding this, that, the other.

"You've gone quiet," said Rachel.

He looked up, saw from the look in her eyes that he'd failed some kind of test.

"You may now kiss the bride."

Miroslav and Rachel looked nervously at each other.

"Go on!" shouted one of the late arrivals, laughing. Miroslav put his arms around her; they almost burst out laughing, then kissed.

"Can we take photos in here?" asked the photographer.

"You can try," replied the registrar, "It is rather dark."

His jaw tightened, he'd meant *is it allowed?* Of course his camera could cope with this light.

"Can you kiss the bride again?" he asked, an edge to his voice now, crouching down in front of them.

"That is one request I am very happy to oblige," said Miroslav, with a huge grin. He kissed Rachel again, then again a minute later, as the others jostled for position, struggling to focus, while Keith and the other witness, Dragica, stood in the corner, signing the clerk's giant ledger.

On the way out, they passed the next wedding party coming down the corridor. Butch lesbian bride, a much smaller, nervous Latin man, his English boyfriend giving his hand a discrete squeeze as they passed.

Rachel and Miroslav walked out of the registry office two, three, four times, giving everyone the opportunity to get a good photo. A passing driver sounded his horn and waved at them.

Keith felt a hand on his shoulder.

"Please."

It was the photographer. He took off his jacket, handed it to Keith.

"Wear this," he said, frowning at his tee shirt. Keith realised he was expected to join the group photographs.

The photos over, Miroslav stepped to the front.

"Please, everyone come to the park and celebrate — it's just across the road."

He nodded at Keith.

"Please join us."

They gathered around a couple of benches near the fountain. Everyone began unpacking the food and drink they'd brought. Sandwiches, samosas, bhajis, crisps, chicken drumsticks were handed round. Miroslav, Dragica and the elderly couple produced bottles of slivovic and plastic glasses from M&S carrier bags.

A couple of clowns walked past, clutching cans of Tenants Extra. They were dressed in outsized tartan suits, wore nametags identifying them as Mr Dipstick and Mr Silly.

"I hate clowns," said the little girl, grabbing a chicken drumstick.

"Sssssh," hissed her mother.

Mr Dipstick farted loudly.

"Ugh, how gross!"

"They're the reason we were so late," said an anxious red haired woman, turning to Rachel and Miroslav. "The traffic along the front was locked solid. Apparently they were having some kind of parade. I don't know what's going on, the place is crawling with them."

"It's the International Clown Festival," said Keith.

They all turned to stare at him.

"Well — it is."

He'd spent all day covering it. In the morning attending the clown's service at St Michael's, the congregation consisting entirely of clowns, the vicar dressing as one for the occasion. In the afternoon he'd mingled with the delegates at The Winter Gardens, interviewing Mr Jolly about his plans to introduce clowns onto children's wards in hospitals, a common practice in America.

Dragica cleared his throat and proposed a toast.

"To Rachel and Miroslav!"

Everyone raised their glass, shouted the toast, threw back their heads. The slivovic burnt Keith's throat, made his eyes

water. When he'd recovered, he walked over to where Rachel
and Miroslav stood. He shook Miroslav's hand, then turned to
Rachel.

"Congratulations."

"Thank you."

"How are you?"

"Fine. And you?"

"Fine."

"Well, that's good."

"So, now we are all friends," said Miroslav.

"Oh my God!"

Rachel gripped the arm-rest, squeezed her eyes shut. The
coach had just veered into the opposite lane again, narrowly
missing oncoming traffic.

"He must be doing eighty," said Keith.

The coach lurched violently back to the left. Branches
clawed at the windows.

Keith checked his watch, it was 11.00 a.m. They were still a
couple of hours from Prague.

"He's been driving non-stop for around twenty-two hours
now."

About an hour into France, the TV showing the tedious
Richard Pryor and Gene Wilder video wrenched itself free of
its brackets, crashed down onto the head of the relief driver,
asleep in the chair underneath. After bandaging his head, the
hostess and second driver had a heated discussion on the hard
shoulder while the passengers watched nervously from the
coach.

What are they saying?

I think he's asking her if she's ever driven a coach.

Eventually they climbed back on board, smiling unnerving-
ly.

"We are now driving to Prague. No problem. Thank you."

At first they'd seen the lighter side of it. Keith crept to the
front of the coach to sneak a look at the wounded man.

"My god, he looks like Basil Fawlty in that episode where
they bandage his head up after the moose falls on it. The one
where he insults the Germans."

A party atmosphere developed. While the hostess was distracted, tending to the injured driver, plying the healthy one with black coffee, the passengers began helping themselves to the bottles of beer from the fridge at the back.

The least we deserve is a few free drinks after this!

Soon the fridge was empty, darkness fell, hysterical laughter broke out as the drunken passengers attempted to inflate their blow up pillows and get to sleep.

Keith and Rachel were woken at seven by the man opposite using his electric razor. In the pale grey light of morning, hungover, stiff, it didn't seem so funny.

"Why hasn't the lunatic stopped for a break?" asked Rachel.

"I think he's frightened that he'll fall asleep if he does, and might never wake up again. He must have drunk about a gallon of black coffee. I don't know where he's putting it."

"I can't believe I agreed to a twenty-four hour coach journey. If we ever do get to Prague I'll take a week to recover. It wasn't *that* much more to fly."

Her remark stung Keith, as it was meant to do. He'd finally got his equity card, three years after leaving RADA, but hadn't worked since his brief appearance in *Minder*, as a flasher in the park, last year. As usual, he was broke.

"You're not the only one worried about money, Keith. I'm not exactly rolling in it."

She'd given up teaching, was a student again, studying law, having decided to train as a solicitor.

The coach crept into the opposite lane again. A car horn blared, a woman at the front of the coach screamed. The coach lurched back to the right.

"We're going to crash," said Rachel very quietly. "We're all going to die."

Keith looked around — the couple behind held hands; an elderly man bowed his head, mumbling prayers; a young woman on her own bit her lip, struggling to hold back the tears. They knew, they all knew, that this was it, their time was up. If they weren't careful, he and Rachel would spend their last moments on Earth bickering. He reached for Rachel's hand.

"I know things haven't been very good between us for a while now, but..."

His eyes filled with tears.

"I love you."

"I love you too," she said, her voice breaking. She leaned forward to kiss him just as the driver slammed on the brakes, jerking them forward, ramming their heads into the back of the seat in front of them.

The red haired woman and Miroslav sat on a bench, talking in lowered voices, their heads bent. Keith walked over to where Rachel was feeding a scabby black dog a chicken drumstick. She stood up, wiped her hands, nodded at Miroslav and the woman.

"That's Sarah, she and Miroslav live together."

"Why did you marry him?"

"Because Sarah couldn't, she's already married to a Colombian."

"So he doesn't have to go back to Colombia."

"Exactly. And now Miroslav doesn't have to go back to Sarajevo."

Keith nodded. He felt his spirits lifting.

"So what are you doing here?"

"I'm writing an article on the International Clown Festival."

He struggled to conceal his delight.

"I've got a regular half page in *The Independent on Sunday*."

He hadn't stopped writing plays, but this *payed!*

She nodded, "I've seen it."

It was called *How Peculiar*. She lit a cigarette.

"I saw that one on The Brucies. Did you actually wear one of those wigs?"

He smiled, "Of course."

The Bruce Forsyth Social Club met once a month to go on a pub crawl. At every pub they charged in, shouting "Nice to see you, to see you *NICE!*" In honour of one of the most famous hair pieces in showbiz, they wore pieces of carpet on their heads — bright blue, red, purple, stripes, whatever offcuts the local carpet fitter could spare.

"What sad people."

Keith had been going to tell her about his encounter with the Test Card Appreciation Society. How he'd attended their convention, watched videos of test cards with them — interesting regional variations, Christmas specials with holly in the corners. But now he reconsidered, disappointed by her reaction.

"You love that kind of thing, don't you? The weirder the better. I think you've finally found your true vocation."

He decided it wasn't a criticism, pressed on.

"How about you? What are you up to?"

"Still a solicitor, in the same practice as Sarah."

"A house by the sea?"

She nodded, "Uhuh."

"Rachel."

Sarah was beckoning her to the bench.

"I'll be back in a minute."

Keith watched her go. He was so happy for her — she had her house by the sea, and now both of them were finally doing well. What a brilliant stroke of luck for him to have found her again. He thought of something Miroslav had said to him earlier.

In my language, we have the same word for luck and happiness.

He drained his glass, the slivovic didn't burn his throat any more, it filled him with a warm glow. He'd move in, they'd start a family, have Miroslav and Sarah round for dinner every week. The scabby mutt looked up at him with pleading eyes. They'd have a dog too, and take it for long walks along the clifftop. He found a half-eaten sandwich in his pocket, gave it to him.

"I don't want to live like this anymore," said Rachel.

They sat at the kitchen table. They were living in a short-life housing co-op in Hackney.

"I work hard, I want to come back to somewhere nice at the end of the day."

Warning bells began ringing in Keith's head.

"It's not that bad," he said unconvincingly.

"Oh yeah, it's wonderful. Look at you, sitting there with your eyebrows singed off."

That morning, the pilot light on the ancient water heater had gone out again, Keith had foolishly left the hot tap running when relighting it. Flames shot out, removing his eyebrows.

But Keith thought this place had its good points too. The rent was only £5 a week, and he could play his music as loud as he liked while he worked.

"Rachel, you're tired, you need..."

"Don't tell me I'm tired. I know I'm tired, I've just been deal-
ing with immigration cases all night at the law centre. It's not
just that. It started pouring with rain as I left work, and I knew
if you were home you'd be running around our bedroom, putting out bowls and saucepans trying to catch the leaks, and
that if you were out the bed would be fucking wet again. And
I thought 'Why am I putting myself through this when I don't
have to?'"

Keith noticed a mouse scurrying past the bin, but he didn't
mention it.

"I want to live somewhere nice, where there aren't any
leaks, where there's no danger of being gassed, that has an
inside toilet, where the neighbours don't keep a bloody goat in
the back garden."

"But this place has got character."

She ignored him.

"Far away from Hackney, someplace where I don't feel like
I'm the only normal person on the streets. It wears you down,
feeling like that."

"But..."

"The streets? What am I talking about? It'd be a relief to feel
I'm not the only normal person in the house!"

She touched her forehead delicately with her fingers.

"I've got a bloody great lump from banging into the wall
after tripping over the Starship Enterprise again on the way
out this morning."

Kirsty, the woman who had the downstairs bedroom, went
everywhere with an enormous metal model of the Starship
Enterprise on a rope around her neck. The first thing she did
when getting home was take it off and leave it in the hall, desperate to shed the weight.

"If you got a job, we could look for a place of our own."

Keith froze in terror; soul-destroying job, mortgage, kids, he
and Rachel turning into souped-up versions of their parents.
Up in the loft, damp and forgotten, his plays. His last one had
gone out on Radio 3 a few months ago. Despite writing dozens
of letters with false names and addresses to *Pick of the Week*,
there'd been a disappointing lack of positive feedback. Still,
he'd just sent another off to *The Gate*. It only needed one phone

call to transform everything.

We loved your play, can we meet for lunch?

He'd faked a rent book, allowing him to claim £30 a week. He still got the odd repeat fee for some adverts he'd done eighteen months ago. It wasn't a fortune, but it was enough to get by till he made it. Destroy the tender sapling of his talent for a few measly extra quid a week?

"Well..." said Keith, "You've obviously had a bad day, you look like you've got a headache, it must be freaking you out seeing me without any eyebrows..."

Rachel took a deep breath, placed both hands on the table in front of her.

"I know you think you're preserving your precious freedom by steering clear of anything that might tie you down, but in fact you've become so frightened of change that, *inside*, you're just as tied down as someone with four kids and a mortgage. You're *stuck*, Keith."

She shook her head.

"This is it, I can't take any more of this kind of life. I'm going to start looking for a flat in a decent area. I'd like you to come with me. What do you say?"

She astonished him. She knew so clearly what she wanted from life! Keith had never managed such a thing, always seeing himself from the outside when he tried to act decisively. The knack of becoming completely absorbed in his life eluded him.

"Well?"

"I don't know. I need time to think."

"Do you want to go for a drink? Someplace we can talk."

"I should get back."

"Come on, we haven't seen each other for years, can't you spare half an hour?"

Rachel hesitated, biting her lip.

"I feel we both need to think about this. Why don't you go back home, and if you feel the same way in a couple of days, give me a ring."

"OK," he took a notepad from his shoulder bag, opened it, pleased with how crisp and business-like his actions were. He clicked the top of his pen.

"What's your number?"

*

On Sunday morning, Keith took the tube into central London. He liked to spend a couple of hours wandering from place to place, seeing how many people he could spot reading *How Peculiar*. He settled himself in a little cafe off Long Acre. Across from him a young couple shared *The Independent on Sunday*, the man reading the sports section, the woman the magazine. Suddenly the woman smiled, leaned across to the man.

"Did you know there was a Peashooting World Championship?"

"Oh, this must be whatsisname."

The man lowered the sports page, ready to be amused. The woman read him out the opening sentence.

"'There was controversy this year when one of the competitors strapped a very expensive laser-optic sight, of the kind used by snipers, onto his shooter.'"

They both laughed. Keith sipped his cappuccino, felt a warm glow spreading inside him. How astonished they'd be to discover that the writer of *How Peculiar* was sitting just a few feet away. But it was enough just to witness their reaction. Enough to make his day, in fact.

He rang Rachel the next evening, at eight. He thought that was an excellent time; too early and he'd look frantic; too late and she'd suspect him of dithering.

"Hi Rachel, it's me."

"Oh hi!"

She sounded relaxed and refreshed, as if she'd just stepped out of the shower. He imagined her with just a towel wrapped tightly around her, felt himself harden.

"Well, it's been a couple of days."

"Uh huh."

She was leaving the ball firmly in his court. Well, OK.

"*I* still feel the same. Would you like to meet on Saturday? I could get a train down there, say late afternoon, and we could go for something to eat. How does that sound?"

"Why don't I come up to London?"

"That would be great."

"Actually, I haven't been to London for ages, I wouldn't

mind a look around the shops in the afternoon."

"I could meet you."

"No, I'm sure you'll be busy..."

"No, no. I'm free the whole weekend. I'd *like* to."

"OK, hang on, I'm looking at a timetable now... there's a train that gets into Victoria at half one."

"I'll be there."

"Let's go get a coffee."

She stepped back from him.

"What's the matter?"

"There's a place."

He gestured towards Costa Coffee.

"Don't *do* that."

"What?"

"Ignore what I've just said."

He sighed, ran his hand through his hair.

"I've got to go to Amsterdam this evening."

"You're kidding."

She was going to lose her temper there, in the middle of the concourse, he could see.

"Look, I only just found out about this an hour ago. The editor wants me to go there to see a production of *Hamlet*, and interview the director."

"You're doing *theatre reviews* now?"

"It's an unusual production. The cast are Alsatians. I put the idea to the editor weeks ago, he didn't seem interested at the time. Then, this morning I get a call out of the blue... tonight's the last performance, there's a plane at 4.30 from Stanstead."

She was staring past his shoulder, looking as if she'd just seen something she wished she hadn't.

"I've got to go, it's work."

"Do you?"

She turned her head to look at him, narrowing her eyes.

"Really?"

"That's the way it is with these people. Everything's always decided at the last minute, you never know where you are. It's chaos..."

She held her head in her hands.

"I don't believe this. After all this time... how I could I have

been so stupid?"
   He stretched out his hand towards hers.
   "Don't!"
   "Rachel, please... you're here now, let's get some lunch."
   She thrust her hands deep into her pockets.
   "Goodbye Keith. Enjoy your doggy Hamlet."
   She turned round, started to walk back the way she'd come.

Keith sat in the cafe overlooking the runway. The last performance of the canine *Hamlet* was next weekend, but he'd already
arranged to visit the annual convention of the George Formby
Appreciation Society at the Winter Gardens in Blackpool then,
and he wasn't going to miss *that*!
   It had been hard lying to Rachel but he knew, in the end, that
it was the right decision. The real pleasures in life were small.
Golden nuggets discovered after an age spent sifting through
crap. The things that people promised would bring you happiness were impossible, actually, when you came down to it, to
ever get right. Once he'd finally accepted that, things had
become a lot easier.
   He *liked* his life, didn't feel he was wasting it or missing out.
In a few hours he would be sitting in a theatre in Amsterdam,
watching an Alsatian playing Hamlet, how many people got
the chance to do that?
   It was time to board. One last time he checked to see he had
everything he needed — boarding pass, ticket, passport. He
was ready to go.

A SIMPLE LIFE

It started with a letter from Ireland. Aunt Kathleen wrote to my mother, complaining about how ill she was, asking her to come and look after her. For a few weeks anyhow. Her poor auld sister who never usually asked her for anything.

"How can I say no?" she asked my father, "She's suffering terrible with her nerves. Des is away at sea, she's stuck there on her own with five kids."

"Jesus, Des is no fool, he's well out of it."

Mam narrowed her eyes. There was a short, jagged silence. Then dad waved his hand angrily at her, as if she was a wasp coming too close.

"Go on, go on. You run over there after her, and leave your husband to fend for himself. Jesus what a carry on."

He walked out, muttering. I heard the sharp scrape of the axe being dragged over concrete, then a series of dull, heavy thuds as he started chopping wood. In between each thud I could make out a grunt. The grunts turned to shouts.

Clare ran in, her cheeks flushed.

"Mammy, mammy. Daddy's swearing again."

I hated going to Kathleen's. She spent all day listening to Patsy Cline records, while her kids pulled the place apart around her. The house reeked of stale fried food and pine air freshener. I was 12 that year. I'd have had to share a room with Phil, who was 7, and Liam, 5. Liam wet the bed, Phil barked in his sleep.

It was the beginning of the summer holidays, I wanted to spend them at home, in Wales.

"I don't want to go mam. I want to stay here."

She looked shocked.

"You're coming with me and Clare."

I asked her again in front of dad.

"I've told you once, you're coming with me and Clare."

"What the divil's wrong with you woman, can't you see he doesn't want to go?"

It was the first time in years I'd disagreed with her in front of dad. I forced down the guilt, rising up like castor oil in my throat. I couldn't meet her eyes when I spoke again.

"Why do I have to go? Why can't I stay here with dad?"

He glared at her.

"Aren't you taking the girl already? Jesus Christ, do you have to drag the whole family over to your bloody sister's?"

"Don't you..."

He started roaring.

"Let him stay here if he wants. It'll do him good. It's about time he got free of your apron strings."

The night before she left, mam came up to my room. Things had been tense between us since she'd told me I could stay in Wales with dad. I was lying on my bed, updating my *Shoot!* league tables, listening to *Abbey Road*.

"Do you mind if I turn this down for a minute?"

She asked very politely, I knew then she wasn't going to tell me off. She sat down on the edge of the bed, pressed two pound notes into my hand.

"Get yourself something nice."

I could feel the blood rush to my cheeks. I mumbled my thanks. She handed me a piece of paper.

"That's Pat Doyle's number. You know Pat, he owns the garage down the road from Kathleen. If you tell him that you want to speak to me, he'll send one of the lads down to get me."

She touched my arm gently with her fingers.

"Be sure to give me a ring now, won't you? Just to let me know how you're getting on."

"Yes mam."

"I hope you're going to be alright stuck here on your own with your father."

She picked up the cover of *Abbey Road*, frowned, then put it down again. Neither of us said anything for a while. Mam pulled at a loose thread on the bedspread.

"He can't help it you know. All the Ryans are like that."

She patted my hand, stood up, ready to leave.

"Keep an eye on him for me. "

The next day, waving goodbye to mam and Clare as the boat train to Fishguard pulled away, I began to feel uneasy. They looked so sad and worried leaning out of the window, like a couple of refugees.

I'd hardly ever spent any time on my own with my father before.

When I looked around he had a strange smile on his face.

"You didn't fancy going with them?"

"No."

He started laughing.

"Jesus I'll bet you didn't. Stuck in that miserable house with two prattling women and six screaming kids. Fecking hell, a fate worse than death."

There was a glint in his eye.

"We'll soon sort the place out now the women are out of the way."

He nudged me.

"Come on."

I struggled to keep up with him as he marched down the platform, arms swinging, head held high, humming *Old Skibereen*.

I couldn't remember the last time I'd seen him in such a good mood.

When we got back home, the first thing my father did was rush into the kitchen, and fling open the cupboard doors.

"Come here."

He nodded at the lower shelf.

"Just look at that. How many times must I tell her?"

We stared at the row of tins. He grabbed the nearest one, held it up and read what it said on the label.

"Baked beans in tomato sauce with four frankfurter sausages. This is the kind of muck she buys when my back's turned."

He hurled it into the bin.

THUMP!

"Fecking rubbish."

Mam had stocked up on tinned food before she left, worried

in case we might run out while she was away.

He picked up the next one.

"Spaghetti in... more tomato sauce."

THUMP!

Next.

"Jesus, now I've seen everything. Will you look at this? A tin of spuds."

He shook his head.

"Oh god, they'd fall about laughing if they saw this at home. I'll bet they've never heard tell of an Irish woman buying spuds in tins."

He held it at arm's length, slowly turning it round in his hand.

"When I was growing up in Ireland we may have been poor but by god we ate good, fresh food. We grew our own spuds and vegetables, and caught our own fish. We were never ill. I keep telling your mother not to bring any more tins into this house. Will she listen?"

THUMP!

"I read in the paper the other week about a fella from Pontypool finding a slug in a tin of peas. I made your mother read it. I thought it would make her realise what a fecking hazard these fecking tins are. But no."

He reached up and handed me down the next tin.

"What's that one?"

I read the label.

"Tomato soup."

He nudged me.

"Go on."

I chucked it in the bin.

"Good man! That's the way. You cannot reason with your mother, she'd buy anything. If she sees something advertised on the television, she's got to have it. The one-eyed goggle box has her completely hypnotised."

He picked up the next tin.

"What's this? Peaches in syrup."

He paused, running his eyes over the picture on the label.

"We'll keep that one."

He pushed the tin of peaches to the back, examined the space he'd made in the cupboard.

"Well," he said, looking pleased with himself, "That's a start anyhow. By god I'll have this place sorted out by the time she gets back. She won't recognise it."

Dad cooked the dinner in a frenzy, darting through clouds of steam, singing *Old Skibereen*.

Oh son I loved my native land with energy and pride
Till a blight came o'er my crops, my sheep, my cattle died
My rent and taxes were too high, I could not them redeem
And that's the cruel reason I left old Skibereen.

He drained the spuds, then mixed in diced onions along with the liquid they'd been boiled in. Next he added milk, butter and salt. He brought the big saucepan over to the table. It was no bother to him. Mam struggled to lift it using both hands, she had to wrap a tea towel around the metal handle so she wouldn't burn herself. But dad lifted it easily with one hand, no tea towel, no fuss.

He began dishing out the food. It looked like a great mound of thick, steaming cream had settled on my plate. He sat down, looking very pleased with himself.

"Is this all there is?" I asked.

He gave me a sharp look.

"You're getting very bold, aren't you? Is that all you can say after your own father's just made you a grand dinner?"

He filled his own plate, put the saucepan in the middle of the table, and sat down.

"Is this all there is indeed! What else do you need? Sure didn't the Irish live on spuds, milk and eggs for hundreds of years? There were no tins in those days. And weren't they bursting with health? Didn't they go out and work in the fields all day long, rain, wind or shine on what you're eating now? Go on boy, get stuck in."

Moving very very slowly and carefully, like one of the Men from Uncle defusing a bomb, I pushed my fork into the creamy mound on my plate, brought some to my lips. It wasn't that bad, but I couldn't imagine eating more than a little bit, unless there was something to go with it.

"How in god's name are you ever going to fill out, picking

at your food like that?"

He began shovelling great scoops into his mouth. I tried another forkful, a little larger than the first. He snorted with laughter.

"That wouldn't fill a mouse."

He reached over and grabbed my bicep.

"Jesus, you're like Olive Oil."

"Don't!"

I tried to shrug him off, but he was far too strong for me, he probably could have lifted me up using one hand if he'd wanted.

He held on for a few seconds longer, pushing his thick fingers into my puny muscles, grinning at me, before he let go. My arm throbbed where he'd grabbed it, but I ground my teeth, determined not to show how much it hurt.

"We'll have to start feeding you spinach."

Popeye ate his spinach from a tin.

He shovelled another forkful into his gob.

"I see I have my work cut out. Your mother's spoilt you. She has you soft."

He pointed his knife at me.

"Begob I'll soon toughen you up."

As usual dad woke me up at quarter to six every morning rushing down the stairs, noisily clearing his throat. My bedroom was right above the bathroom, even with the pillow held over my head I heard him grunting and straining on the toilet, then banging and crashing saucepans and bowls in the kitchen as he made porridge. But now when he left for work at half-past-six, with no mam or Clare to disturb the peace I could take the pillow off my head, turn over and go back to sleep.

It was half past nine when I woke up again. Having the house to myself was brilliant. I had Radio One on at top volume. To cut down on washing up I ate the cornflakes straight from the packet, swigging from the bottle of milk in between handfuls. I stayed in the bath for an hour, reading a book about the most decisive battles of World War 2.

Afterwards I called round to Terry's house, Neil was already there. We carried on with our Subbuteo tournament. Terry's dad had nailed the pitch to a piece of hardboard so that it didn't ruck up when you leant on it to play a shot. Terry's mam made us lunch, beans and sausages on toast.

After lunch we walked up to the park. There was always a game of football going on up there, anyone could join in, sometimes there'd be twenty or thirty on each side. When the game was over we bought ice creams and walked up the town centre, wandered around the shops. I had to leave at four to get back and start the dinner. On the way home I bought saveloy and chips so I wouldn't have to eat too much of the dinner at home.

It took Dad nearly an hour to cycle back from the steelworks. He was tired and irritable when he arrived, and having to help make his own dinner made him worse. He didn't say anything when he came in first, just walked over to the sink and washed his face and hands. Then he dried himself, and used the towel to wipe the back of his neck where he'd been sweating.

"How long have the spuds been on?"

"About ten minutes."

"Start the cabbage."

He opened the fridge and took out the bacon. He put it in a bowl and stuck the bowl on top of a saucepan to reheat it. I hated boiled bacon and cabbage, it was even worse when it was reheated the second day.

The kitchen was small, I was careful to avoid bumping into him, in case he lost his temper. I got to know his movements well, could tell when he was going to reach out and turn on the tap, or step back to get something from one of the drawers, and move out of his way just in time. Sometimes I only just avoided colliding with him, and the stench of sweat and oil from his overalls nearly made me heave.

All the time I could hear him thinking *My dinner should be on the table waiting for me when I get in.*

He jabbed the cabbage angrily with a fork, lifted out a piece and tasted it.

"It's ready," he waved me away. "Stand back in case you get scalded, I don't want to be be rushing up to the hospital with you screaming and bawling. Stand back I said."

I couldn't go back any further without leaving the kitchen.

He disappeared in a cloud of steam as he drained the spuds

and cabbage. The reheated bacon had turned bright pink, curling up at the edges. It lay sweating on our plates, licked by the stream of dark green water oozing from the piles of sour cabbage lying next to it. A mountain of spuds filled the rest of the plates. He took some pages from yesterday's paper, laid them down on the chair before he sat on it, to prevent staining it.

He'd poured some of the cabbage water into a cup and now he knocked it back in one, licked his lips and wiped his mouth with the back of his hand. He threw back his head and belched.

"Grand."

We ate in silence. When mam and Clare were there, Clare would be banging her heels against the legs of her chair and humming. Mam would talk non-stop, telling Clare to sit up straight, asking me about what kind of day I'd had in school, telling dad about some piece of gossip she'd heard. Dad would only ever nod his head, or mutter "Aha."

"Aha."

"Aha."

"Aha."

Once he said "Aha" when no one had said anything to him and mam made Clare leave the table because she couldn't stop giggling.

But if Clare was making too much noise, then he'd roar at my mother, "Can't you keep that one quiet?" That was always enough to make Clare, and mam, shut up till the meal was over.

Now there were just the two of us I wondered if I should bring my book to the table and read. It would help to have something to concentrate on, something to block out the loud chomping sounds and heavy breathing coming from the other side of the table.

I went and got my book on *The Decisive Battles of World War 2*. Dad didn't look up when I left the table, or when I came back; he must have heard me turning the pages, but he never said anything. When he'd cleared his plate he leaned back in his chair, belched and said "It's grand and peaceful without the women, isn't it?"

On Friday, a letter came from Ireland.

"Grub first," said dad when I told him, and left it on the

mantelpiece where I'd put it that morning. All through dinner I wondered what my mother had to say. Was Kathleen any better?

Would they be coming back soon? I thought of mam and Clare's sad faces as they left on the train.

When we'd finished eating, dad took the letter from the mantelpiece, sat down in his chair and started reading it out.

"Kathleen is in a bad way. Some days she can't drag herself out of bed at all, she just lies there, crying. Doctor O'Brien's never seen anything like it before."

He laughed to himself.

"Jesus, I'll bet he hasn't."

He took a swig from his cup of tea, looked at me and raised his eyebrows, as if we were both in on the joke together.

"I'm at my wit's end trying to control the kids. Please god she'll get better soon, and we'll be able to come home. I can't give you any idea of how long we'll have to stay, it just depends on how things go with Kathleen."

I waited for him to say something, but he just shook his head and turned to the next page. "Please write and let me know how you're getting on, and ask Michael to give me a ring."

He gave me an odd look over the page.

"Don't forget to pay the bills — underlined twice!"

He cursed under his breath.

"Christ how do you like that? She runs off to Ireland and expects me to stay here and take care of everything *AND* go to fecking work. Don't forget to pay the milkman, don't forget to pay the Life Insurance, don't forget to pay the man from Edwards."

He shot me an angry look.

"Who the feck is Edwards anyhow?"

"We got the three piece suite from them."

"And Williams?"

"The carpet."

"TV Rentals..."

"Mam's payed that for the next couple of months."

She'd taken care of it because you had to go up the town to the office to pay them, all the others came to the door for their money.

He bent over the letter again, read out the next bit.

"The paying-in books are in the hall, I've left the first week's money next to them. They'll call round of a Friday evening. Fecking hell, can I never get any peace?"

He went and got the books, started looking through them.

"Four and sixpence a week... five shillings a week... seven and eleven a week... Jesus, no wonder we're always broke."

He flung the books down on the sofa.

"This HP lark is a fecking con. By the time you've finished paying for something on HP, you've bought the fecker ten times over. How many times have I told her? No more HP, no more fecking insurance, cut down on bills, do you think I'm made of money?"

There was a knock on the door. Dad scowled.

"Here they come, the bastards. Like vultures hovering over a wounded man."

He went and answered it.

"Aha! You must be *Mister* Ryan. Good evening sir, how are you? I'm from Edwards," the man said in a sing-song voice.

Dad started roaring.

"So you're the man from Edwards are you? You fecking blood sucker. You may impress the women with your fancy suit and your nice smile but you don't fool me, oh no. Well you're not getting any more money from this house, so you can piss off out of it."

There was a pause, while the man recovered.

"I have to warn you sir, if you stop the payments, we'll have to take the goods back."

"Take them, take the fecking lot. See if I care."

"This is much better," said Dad, "Christ we should have done this years ago."

We were sitting on a couple of wooden boxes he'd got from the greengrocer's. They were all we had to sit on now, a van from Edwards had come and taken the three piece suite away the day before.

He sat with his back ramrod straight, his hands resting on his knees, looking pleased with himself.

"Those chairs were too soft anyhow, they were bad for you. They'd ruin your back. You'd end up like the fecking

Hunchback of Notre Dame if you sat in those yokes too long."

He slapped the side of the box with the palm of his hand.

"These boxes are much better for you. They make you sit up straight. And that carpet was a waste of money. Jesus you'd never keep a carpet clean in this house, with kids forever trailing muck in after them on their shoes, and your mother dropping cigarette ash everywhere."

Men from Williams had come and rolled up the carpet and taken it away on Monday morning. Dad brought home a couple of bags of sand and spread them over the bare floor.

"This is just how it was at home, years ago. No one could afford carpets in those days. You'd go down to the strand, fill a sack with sand and chuck it over the floor. People nowadays think the old timers were backward."

He snorted and raised his eyebrows, he knew better.

"They weren't so backward at all. Sand is much better than a carpet for floors, it soaks up whatever's spilled on it, and then you just brush it all up and put some more down."

He spat onto the floor.

"Look at that. See how the sand soaks it up? Go on, you have a go."

"No thanks."

He looked disappointed.

"There's no need to spend all that money on carpets and soft auld furniture, the old ways are the best. The old, simple ways."

I lay on my bed, eating a jam doughnut. My father had gone to the allotment. He was usually in a good mood in the evenings now, after he'd had his dinner and bath. He never asked about what I did or where I went in the day. As long as the spuds were ready when he got back, and I didn't bother him while he was eating, he seemed satisfied. He never nagged me about going to bed either, like my mother did. Around half ten he'd say "That's it, Gerry is clocking off for the day" and go upstairs, carrying the huge tin potty he put under the bed. Never a word about not staying up too late. Often I'd watch the telly till the programmes ended and wait till the beginning of the drum roll that signalled the national anthem before jumping up and switching it off.

He gave me money to do the shopping while he was at work; I always kept some of the change for myself, he didn't have any idea of how much things cost so it was easy to fool him. I used it to buy food that I liked. I'd hidden Mars Bars, Marathons, Topics, Kit Kats, Milky Ways, Rolos, Flakes, Galaxys, crisps and Ritz crackers under the bed.

Pat Doyle's number was tucked into my Tottenham Hotspur Football Annual, I took it out and looked at it every now and then, wondering if I should ring my mother and tell her what he'd done? But then I'd imagine the huge row they'd have when she came back. They'd both blame me. Dad for telling on him, mam for not telling sooner. Then I'd get annoyed about mam blaming me when she'd gone off to Ireland and left me with him. But soon I'd start thinking how much better it was in some ways without her and Clare here. Dad was unpredictable, but he didn't keep on nagging me about not going to bed too late, or keeping my room tidy.

In the end, my head would be spinning from the effort of trying to decide what to do. I'd fold the piece of paper up again, put it back in the book, get some more chocolate from under the bed.

I held the sacks open and kept watch while dad shovelled the sand into them. It was dark, but my father said you never knew who might be watching. When we'd finished, we lifted the sacks into the wheelbarrow; dad stood looking around the building site.

"This was all fields and grass once. Hard to believe, isn't it?"

It was.

"They'll never stop till they've covered everything in fecking concrete. In a few years every last square inch of ground will be built on. There'll be nowhere to go if you want a bit of peace and quiet."

We started back, him pushing the wheelbarrow, me walking ahead with the torch, lighting the way.

We cut through the back lanes. The uneven dirt surface and the weight of the wheelbarrow forced dad to go slowly.

"Do you like living in a town?"

"It's OK."

"Ah sure I suppose it's alright if you don't know any better, but if you grew up in the countryside like me... When I was your age, on a fine summer's evening like this I'd like nothing better than to walk down to the sea, sit on the clifftop and watch the dolphins play. Oh Jesus they were grand, I'd spend hours watching them. It was fantastic altogether the way they'd leap right out of the water, twisting and turning."

He stopped, let go of the wheelbarrow and rolled his finger round and round in the air, following it with his eyes as if it was a real dolphin, smiling to himself. I tried to picture him as a boy, but no matter how hard I tried I couldn't conjure up the image; he refused to shrink to my size. He gripped the handles and we set off again.

"Of course if you wanted to see wild animals today, you'd have to get a train to the zoo and pay for the privilege of spending the whole day crushed together with a bunch of gawking eejits. There'd be some kid dripping ice cream down your good trousers, bleddy women blathering in your earhole and fecking teenagers wandering round in a daze with transistors stuck to their ears, 'Yeah Yeah Yeah' blaring out. Oh Christ, no thanks."

He looked at me accusingly, as if I was trying to force him to take me to a zoo.

"You or your sister might enjoy that kind of thing now, but it wouldn't impress me at all."

When we joined Pillgwenlly Road I put the torch away. The Royal Oak was packed, people were jamming the doorway and spilling onto the pavement. Dad's expression darkened at the sound of the raised voices and loud music coming from the juke box. Some of the people on the pavement turned and stared at us as we walked past, obviously wondering what was in the wheelbarrow.

"Why can't people mind their own fecking business?" muttered dad.

We turned down our road.

"Ah no, if you grew up in the countryside you'd never really be happy in a town. Always breathing in petrol fumes, factories pumping muck into the air — you'd put out clean washing in the morning and it'd be dirty again by the evening before you'd even taken it off the line. Tiring your feet out walking on auld concrete all the day, stepping in dogshit. And you'd have to be a madman to go up town of a night. You'd be subjecting yourself to all kinds of indignity. Fellas roaring and shouting, staggering about mad with beer, you'd never know when one of them might go for you, or spew up all over your clothes. The women are just as bad. Plastered in war paint, shrieking and swearing at the top of their voices, completely out of control, no bit of shame at all. Oh Christ, don't talk to me about towns. There's no bit of peace and contentment to be had in a town at all. I don't envy you, growing up here. God knows what the world will be like by the time you're my age. Well thanks be to Jesus I won't have to worry about it anyhow, I'll be six feet under by then, it won't be my problem any more. You'll have to manage the best you can without me."

When we got home, we emptied one of the sacks over the floor, and spread it around, then stood the others in the hall-way. It was nearly half-past-ten by the time we'd finished, and dad got ready for bed. When he'd finished in the bathroom, he came out carrying the potty, paused in the doorway before going upstairs.

"We get on grand, don't we?"

I didn't know what to say.

"There were eleven of us. You meet people nowadays who say large families are a great thing. Well don't you believe them. It was fecking awful. We were always fighting, there was never enough to go round you see. Jesus I wish the father had tied a fecking knot in it."

His voice thickened.

"My father would never sit down and talk to me the way I do to you. He'd give you a belt round the side of the head as soon as look at you. Oh God you don't know how lucky you are."

Suddenly he looked embarrassed, and straightened his shoulders.

"That's it, Gerry is clocking off for the day."

Another letter came from Ireland. After dinner, we went into the living room, sat down on our boxes with our mugs of tea. Dad ripped open the letter and started reading it out.

"Kathleen's still no better. Ha! I'd soon cure her. A poke in the head with a sharp stick first thing in the morning, and she'd soon be up and getting the breakfast ready."

He reached up to the mantelpiece for his mug, took a slurp of tea.

"I'm still waiting for a letter from you... why doesn't Michael give me a ring? The weather here is very changeable, you never know where you are, it's sunny one day, overcast the next... Blah blah blah... Jesus the same auld rubbish, your mother writes a terrible letter."

He turned over the page.

"The way things are going, we may have to stay till August, when Des gets back from sea."

August!

Dad read the next bit silently, shaking his head.

"Don't forget to pay the rates — underlined of course."

He screwed up his face.

"More fecking money. And where does it go? Straight into the pockets of some fella up in the town hall. This is a terrible country for bills and rates and fecking official letters and rules and regulations. You know, before you were born I wanted to move to Australia, to go live in the outback, away from all their fecking rules and regulations, but your mother wouldn't have it. Ah no, says she, it's too far away from me family. It's too hot. I couldn't stand them kangaroos, they're like great big rats hopping about all over the place, they'd frighten you to death. Have you ever heard such rubbish, do you see what I have to put up with?"

He got up from his box and chucked the letter into the fireplace, then took his socks down from the mantelpiece and continued with the darning he'd started last night. He'd got rid of all the nick-nacks mam used to keep there — the china cats and dogs, the little windmill. The only things on the mantelpiece now were a hammer, some nails, a sharp knife, his nail-file.

"I'd definitely advise you not to get married, Michael. You're better off doing your own washing and cleaning in the end, even though it's the last thing you'd feel like doing at the end of a hard day's work. And for companionship, get yourself a dog. For god's sake, don't make the same mistake I did. Stay single. A wife and kids would always drag a fella down."

*

"Turn off the electric light," he said in a hushed voice, his eyes shining with excitement. I did, and then the only light in the room came from the lamp and the coal fire, and the moon shining through the window. It was really nice.

"It's just like the auld days back home, before anyone had electricity."

I went and stood next to him.

"There's a lovely soft, warm glow to it, isn't there?" he said, nodding at the lamp, his voice still hushed. "Grand and soothing."

"Yes, it is," I replied, keeping my voice low too.

We stood together, looking at the flame flickering in the lamp, the silence warm and comforting around us. He'd bought it in the market that day, and before he even tried it out, was talking about putting one in every room.

"You'd get sick of that harsh auld electric light burning right into your eyes. It'd blind you, Christ you'd feel you were being interrogated — 'Achtung! You are our prisoner Paddy. There is no escape. It will be better for you if you talk now.'"

He'd tied a fork to the end of the spare poker with wire, so that you could make toast over the fire without burning your hands. He put a slice of bread on the end of it now, and we drew up our boxes in front of the fire and watched him toast it.

"I think it's the years of exposure to electric light that's made your mother so irritable. When I first met her back home, she was a very cheerful person, believe it or not. She's not used to the glare of the electric bulb you see, she never had to deal with them till she was nigh on twenty. Oh yes, I've been giving the matter of your mother's sourness some serious thought. Electric light, the one-eyed goggle box and tinned food — those are the main suspects. That side's done."

It was lovely and brown, he turned it over.

"Would you like some stout?"

I must have looked surprised, he frowned and said, "Is it fourteen you are now, or fifteen?"

"Twelve."

He looked at me doubtfully.

"Go and get a couple of mugs why don't you? And bring the sugar."

When I came back from the kitchen he handed me the toasting fork.

"There, you have that one."

While he went to the pantry to get the stout, I walked over to the table and buttered the toast. The first crunching bite, with the butter still melting on it, was gorgeous. I stuck another slice on the fork and started toasting that one. Dad came back with two bottles. He opened one and poured it into the mugs, carefully tilting the bottle, controlling the flow. His face was creased with concentration, he moved very slowly, like a man handling nitro-glycerine. When he'd finished, he put a spoonful of sugar in each and stirred it.

"The Guinness in this country is awful bitter. It's nothing like the nice smooth, creamy pint you'd get at home. You'd have to add some sugar to be able to stick it."

He handed me a mug. It wasn't bad, but still a little bitter. I put a second spoonful of sugar in it. We made some more toast and drank our stout. My head started to swirl.

"This is grand toast, isn't it? You cannot beat toast done over an open fire. Or any food for that matter. That fecking useless Kathleen, she's no idea how to cook at all. All you'd ever get there is a fry up — breakfast, lunch and dinner. Jesus I bet if you handed that one an orange she'd chuck it in the pan and fry it."

I laughed so loud I spilt some of my stout.

"She never changes the lard — she uses the same auld stuff for weeks on end. Months probably."

"Years!" I shouted, laughing.

"You'd have to pity poor Des, he had no idea what he was letting himself in for. He saw her at the ceilidh with her smart clothes on, and her face plastered in war paint and the poor eejit thought he'd met a real beauty queen. By Jesus, I'll bet his jaw dropped the first time he saw her in the morning after she'd scraped that muck off her face and was leaning over the frying pan, coughing like a chimney, a Capstan Full Strength stuck in her gob. She must have looked like something from *The Outer Limits*."

"Like this," I shouted, jumping out of the chair, pulling down my bottom lip and rolling my eyes up into my head.

"Oh god, me nerves are at me."

Dad roared, rocking back and forth on his box, slapping his

leg.

"Good man! Go on, have another drop of stout."

"I will."

I handed him my mug and he filled it again. I could feel myself swaying while I watched him, and I started imagining what it would be like to be at sea for months on end, the waves crashing over the bows, living on toast and stout. He handed me the mug, I sat back down and added some sugar.

"Careful, you're dropping that sugar all over the place."

I brushed it off my sleeve and trousers.

"I like auld Des mind, he's a decent fella. I feel sorry for him, married to that bleddy Kathleen. He should have married that German one he met in Hamburg. You've never seen the likes of German women for work. They're up at the crack of dawn, washing and scrubbing and cleaning. Fair play to the fräuleins, they know how to work all right."

He took another sip, wiped the back of his mouth with his hand.

"August indeed, I doubt if Des will be back in August at all."

He paused, smirking to himself.

"I wonder what your mother will do then? Perhaps she'll stay till Christmas. Let her, I don't care, do you?"

"No," I said, "I don't care either. I don't care if she never comes back," and I took another swig of stout.

Dad stood in the middle of the yard, watching the chickens pick at the feed he'd scattered on the ground.

"Spuds and cabbages from the allotment, fresh eggs from our own chickens — soon we'll hardly need to go to the shops at all. No need for fancy modern conveniences, we've got everything we need right here."

He'd bought half a dozen chickens and a cockerel, built a coop in the corner of the garden for them.

"Are you going to open the letter?"

Another letter had arrived from Ireland that morning. Sighing he replied, "Aye I suppose I may as well."

We went inside, he stood next to the fireplace, one arm resting on the mantelpiece while he read it silently.

"What does she say?"

"The same auld rubbish."

He put it back in the envelope, shoved it into his pocket. I was disappointed, I wanted to know if my mother had said anything about me. Next he opened an official brown envelope. He read it then screwed it up and chucked it into the fireplace.

"The council wanting money for rates. Final demand indeed. They may scare your mother, but they don't scare me."

There was a knock on the door. Dad was coming down the stairs, humming *Old Skibereen*; he answered it.

"Is Michael in?"

It was Terry's voice.

"He is, come on in lads."

Neil must have been with him. I got up from my box, ready to say hello. Their mouths fell open when they saw the room.

"Hi-ya."

My voice rose too high. I sounded like a frightened girl. They looked away, alarm in their eyes.

Dad nudged them in the back.

"Go on, make yourselves at home. I've just made some tea."

Terry and Neil looked at each other, uncertain what to do. Dad nodded at the boxes.

"Go on, sit down for god's sake."

The blood drained from my face when I saw the look that passed between them. Terry winked at Neil; Neil smirked. They sat down on the boxes. Dad went into the kitchen. Neil pushed some sand around with his shoe.

"I wonder what it's like here when the tide comes in?"

They both burst out laughing. It was as if I didn't exist. Dad came back in with the tea. Dad and I had to stand, there were only two boxes. Dad took his nail file from the mantelpiece and began doing his nails. A couple of chickens wandered in from outside. Terry noticed the bucket full of potato peelings, scraps of bread and tea slops standing in the corner. He nudged Neil, nodding at it; they both started giggling. Terry spilt some of his tea.

"Sorry."

"Ah don't worry about it, it'll soon dry out. We're not very grand here, are we Michael?"

"Shall we go out?"

Dad looked at me as if I'd gone mad.

"What's wrong with you? They've only just got here."

Outside, the cockerel started crowing. Dad frowned.

"Ah the fecking eejit anyhow."

It had begun crowing in the evenings instead of the mornings.Terry and Neil began sniggering again. I stared down into my tea, praying that they'd go.

The next morning, instead of calling round to Terry or Neil's house I decided to go straight to the park instead. As I reached the top of Lime Street, the two of them came out of the sweet shop. They looked at each other, laughed, and ran off.

I walked up the town, and got some new books from the library.

"I don't know what's come over you recently. You're always in front of the goggle box. A young fella like you should be bursting with energy, you should be outside, giving me a hand."

I didn't say anything. I didn't want to go outside, I hated the chickens, their glassy eyes and stuttering walk made me feel sick. The neighbours had started complaining about the cockerel. They were right, it was mad keeping one in a house.

"What is this?"

"Top of The Pops."

The Rolling Stones had just made it to number one with *Jumping Jack Flash*. My father scowled at the screen.

"God almighty, it sounds like tom cats screeching. Look at the size of that fecker's gob, he's like an ape."

I could feel him watching me, but I didn't react.

"You can tell that one's never had to work for a living. A day's work'd kill him. He'd be bawling after half an hour — 'Oh god I'm dying, me hands are raw. I can't lift this shovel anymore, it's too heavy for me.'"

He moved right in front of the telly, blocking the view.

"Jesus is there no end to the rubbish they put on television these days? You'd think they'd manage to put something decent on once in a while. A good ceilidh now, or some Irish dancing, or one of those documentaries about wild animals — something educational. But no, all you seem to get for your money is a bunch of hairy feckers with great big gobs on them shouting 'yeah yeah yeah.' It'd make you sick so it would."

Now he turned round and faced me, leaning forward so that his head was blocking the screen.

"How is it that someone like me, with no education, can see this lot for what they are and you can't? Eh? Answer me that now."

I looked straight ahead, avoiding his stare.

"I thought as much — you *have* no answer to that one, do you?"

He stood up straight again, and switched the telly off. The Rolling Stones disappeared into the little white dot in the centre of the screen.

I was walking through the town centre, eating a bag of chips when I noticed my father walking towards me, pushing the wheelbarrow. The television was in it. It was a very hot day, he was dressed in his Australian bush hat, white vest, shorts and hobnail boots. He noticed me.

"What are you doing eating that muck?"

"Where are you going with the telly?"

"You'll ruin your stomach with that greasy rubbish. Come on, I'm going to Radio Rentals."

It was just up the street. As we reached the door I asked, "Is it broken?"

"Come on, open the door for me."

People were pointing and sniggering.

There was a lady in a smart blue blazer sitting behind the desk, she looked up as we struggled in with the wheelbarrow.

"Can I help you?"

"You can, take this."

"I beg your pardon?"

He reached into the wheelbarrow, chucked the rental book onto the desk.

"The wife hired it. She's gone back to Ireland now and I'm giving it back to you. I don't want it."

She looked at the book, cleared her throat.

"You agreed to hire it for a minimum period of..."

He started roaring.

"I didn't agree to anything, aren't I telling you it was the wife?"

"I'm afraid you can't just..."

He lifted the telly out of the wheelbarrow. A man in a suit came out of the back room, smoothing down his tie with his hands.

"It's alright Sharon, I'll deal with this. How can I help you sir?"

"You can take this back," said dad, shoving it hard into his chest, so that the man staggered backwards with the shock. My father turned on his heel.

"Get the door," he barked.

We walked back home in silence.

"Doyle's Garage."

It was Pat Doyle, I recognised his voice.

"I want to speak to my mother please — Mrs Ryan. She's staying with her sister Kathleen down the road."

He put the phone down. In the background, someone revved an engine. A country and western song played on the radio. Kathleen's house was a couple of hundred yards down the road, I tried to make my mind go blank while I waited, so that I wouldn't start worrying about dad walking past or the money running out before I could get to speak to my mother. Suddenly I heard her voice on the other end of the phone.

"Hello?"

"Dad's gone beserk, he took the telly back to TV Rentals in a wheelbarow. He got rid of all the furniture because it's bad for your back, and we have to sit on boxes, the carpet's gone too, there's nothing but sand on the floor and he won't pay the bills..."

"Michael is that you?"

Something was wrong.

"Who is this?"

"It's your Aunt Kathleen, your mother went back this morning. She's been worried sick about you, why didn't you give her a ring? And after the terrible things your father said in that letter..."

She started crying.

"I've never seen her so upset, I'm in no state to help her and now I've no one. Oh holy mother of god, what kind of man *is* your father anyhow?"

When I got back, dad was sitting in the living room, cutting his toenails. He smiled when I came in.

"Another grand day, isn't it?"

I nodded, and went and stood by the window, my hands in my pockets.

"I bought you some chocolate, it's there on the mantelpiece."

He nodded at a bar of Galaxy. He'd never bought me chocolate before; I mumbled my thanks.

"You liked the auld goggle box, didn't you?"

He was looking sheepish.

"Perhaps we could pick up a second-hand one for a few quid. It's this HP lark I can't stand you see..."

Through the window I could see a taxi pulling up.

"I'm just going outside for a minute."

As I stepped out through the back door I heard the front gate opening. The chickens scattered as I rushed past. There were three bolts on the back gate, I undid them and stepped down into the back lane.

I started running.

I DREAMT I SAW JOE HILL LAST NIGHT

I'll tell you what kind of place Morecambe is. This afternoon I went into a cafe for a cup of tea. While I was waiting to be served I noticed Ken Dodd's tickling stick proudly displayed in a glass case on the wall. I left straight away. There are limits.

I wandered along the seafront, past the bingo, chips and candyfloss, past Cheap And Cheerful, Krazy Prices and the boarded up shopfronts just beyond. Crossing over by the shabby station I entered that great white relic, the Midland Hotel. Got myself a gin and tonic, found myself a seat in the sun lounge, watched the afternoon run out of steam. As the clouds built up over the peaks of the Lake District across the bay, I couldn't help being reminded of the dimming of one of those long, slow summer days in the Rhondda of my child-hood. Increasingly I find comfort in remembering being some-where else. Someplace I was happy, though if you were to ask me exactly how or why I was happy there, I probably couldn't tell you.

Morecambe is part of my regular summer run, you'll find me here every year. In a couple of hours I'll be taking the stage just down the road in The Bubble, a modern, rather modest venue on the seafront. Last night they had The Bernie Sugden Sextet, tonight it's me, Paul Thomas, tomorrow it's Ken Spragg and his Cheeky Monkey featuring adult material that some people may find offensive.

Hope I can manage "It's really great to be back in Morecambe" without choking on the words, or being struck down by a bolt of lightning. Then I'll let them have it — *I Left My Heart in San Fransisco, For Once in My Life, Save the Last Dance for Me*. That's right, an evening of dangerously avant garde material. About half-past-ten, I'll pull out the handker-chief, mop my brow and tell them how the record shows, that through it all, I took the blows, and did it My Way.

I blame Reg for bringing on this fit of melancholy. He's the Entertainment Correspondent on the local rag (or the Lack of Entertainment Correspondent as I like to call him). This morning, at the end of the interview, he asked me which singer had had the greatest influence on me. That was a bit probing for our Reg, he's not exactly Anthony Clare. At first I thought the sudden burning sensation in my chest must be heartburn, and began searching my pockets for the Rennies. But, after a few seconds, I realised it was regret. *My God*, I thought, *What's all this about, you silly old bugger? Come on now, snap out of it.* Reg was squinting quizzically at me through his permanent cloud of cigarette smoke, waiting for an answer, probably expecting me to say Frank Sinatra, or Tony Bennet, or maybe even, god help me, Harry Secombe. He looked most surprised when I told him it was Paul Robeson. To Reg he was probably just that big black bloke with the deep voice, who sang *Ol' Man River*.

My father idolised Robeson. Ah, dear old dad, someone really should put the old bugger on display.

Roll up! Roll up! Come and see the last of the class warriors.

They'd make a fortune, what a novelty he'd be in these monetarist times. He went down the pit at fourteen, joined the Communist Party at sixteen, fought in the Spanish Civil War. I don't think he's ever forgiven me for abandoning the male voice choir for rock and roll, that crude tool of American imperialism. That's right, you wouldn't think it to look at me now, but I was a bit of a rocker in my time, had my own group, Johnny Dean and The Swingers, otherwise known as Cliff, Ginge, Gog, Speccy and Vernon. By the early Sixties we were getting five bookings a week, at £12 to £15 a night, pretty decent money in those days, especially on top of our day jobs. I was earning three or four times what my father was getting down the pit, playing the kind of music he despised.

The Abercynon Ballroom, the Memorial Hall, Tredegar, the Cwm Welfare, Beddau, Pontypridd YMCA, those were our stomping grounds. Thought we'd be playing them for ever. Despaired of being snapped up by an agent and whisked off to the bright lights, till the lovely Crispin De Courcey approached me one night as I came off stage at the Top Hat club in Cwmtillery. I'd never come across anything like him in the Valleys before; Laurence Harvey would have played him in the film. At first I thought he was going to ask me to call him a cab, or fetch his coat. But instead he said, "You're rather good" in that droll, ironic way of his so that you couldn't tell if you were being complimented or mocked. I turned my face into a mask, determined not to look like the kind of small town boyo who'd be overawed by a toff from London.

"How long have you been performing in clubs?"

"About three and a half years now."

"Really? That long?"

He took a sip of his Martini, arched an eyebrow.

"I'm afraid I rarely get to Wales."

He made it sound as though it were Wales' fault for not insisting he came earlier.

"Do you have a manager?" he asked.

"Well, we..."

"We?"

The Swingers were sitting around a table just behind us, looking as if they were waiting for the Quasimodo look-alike competition to begin. Crispin glanced over his shoulder.

"Oh, you mean *those*."

I shifted uneasily.

"Hmmm. The group scene is pretty crowded at the moment. What I'm *really* looking for is a solo artist."

Cliff and Ginge were my cousins, I'd known the rest of The Swingers since primary school; we all lived within ten minutes of each other. I could feel them all watching us, wondering what was going on.

"I couldn't just walk out on the boys like that."

He weighed me up with his hooded eyes.

"A pity. Still, I'm sure you'll be able to carry on packing them in at places like this for years, no problem."

He checked his watch; terribly corny, but effective.

"Speccy has always fancied himself as a lead singer, I suppose he could take my place."

He nodded encouragingly.

"Yes, why not? A solo career."

"It's a tough market though. We'll need something to catch the public eye."

He looked around him disdainfully, surveying what passed for nightlife in Cwmtillery.

"I think I've come up with an angle."

"What's that then?"

He plucked the slice of lemon from his cocktail stick, sucked it.

"You're Welsh, if I'm not mistaken."

"Uh... yes."

"Don't be embarrassed."

"Who said I was embarrassed?"

But he was already looking beyond me, a glazed look in his eyes that I would later come to recognise as greed.

"Oh yes indeed, you're Welsh, boyo."

He began chuckling to himself.

My first hit, *Working in a Coal Mine*, featured me doing an Elvis-style vocal, backed by a male voice choir. On the record sleeve, I'm dressed as a miner, my face blackened, the winding gear as a backdrop. I was instantly dubbed Nat King Coal. Other hits followed, including rock and roll versions of *Bread of Heaven* and *Men of Harlech*, and, a real collector's item this, a cover of *We'll Keep A Welcome In The Hillsides* with Pinky and Perky, the singing pigs. I took some stick whenever I went home, I can tell you.

Naturally my father wasn't impressed.

"I can't hold my head up in the street anymore, Pinky and bloody Perky."

After a couple of years, I began to record more middle-of-the road numbers like *The Ballad of Tiger Bay*, and *Where Are You Now, Rhondda Boy?* (living in a mock-Elizabethan semi in a Surrey village, just down the road from Engelbert Humperdinck).

What a time that was. I'd get home in the early hours, find Miranda sprawled across our white leather sofa, nine sheets to the wind.

"Well hello Rhondda boy," she'd slur, when she'd finally got me in focus.

"Hello my darling wife, and what have you been up to today?"

"Oh, you know... washing and cleaning, a little embroidery, that sort of thing."

A pity our daughter had to get caught in the middle. Poor Julie, no wonder she was such a precocious child. Sometimes the three of us would be walking along the street when she'd turn to a passer by, crying "Help! These aren't my real parents. I've been kidnapped. Call the police!" Or, if we were visiting friends, she'd stand in the middle of the room and shout, "Mummy had a bottle of gin for breakfast" or once, "Daddy wears a dress at home."

When Miranda and I finally got divorced, it would break my heart to drop her back at at the end of one of my access days. I'd bend down to kiss her cheek, and she'd stare at me with those cool green eyes and say, "I'll never see you again, will I?"

Oh god, here comes the burning sensation again. Steady now, you old bugger, don't panic. Quick, fast forward to the Seventies.

That's when I began to get TV work. Good old Crispin, he got me a regular spot on the panel game *On the Tip of My Tongue*. The format was simple, they'd play a brief extract from an old song, and the contestants had to sing the next line. I ran up bonus points with jokes about Welsh rarebits, sheep, leeks and lines like "Llanfairpwllgwyngyllgogerychwyrndrobwlllantysiliogogogoch — so good they named it fifteen times."

When it was finally axed in '79, I struggled, I have to admit. Did some day-time TV, secured the odd appearance on *Blankety Blank*, but was soon reduced to singing on cruise liners and...

Oh Christ!

I've just had a panto flashback.

Six weeks as one of the Ugly Sisters in Torquay.

There's only one known cure for Panto flashback, and that's a stiff drink. I make my way to the bar.

"Hello Mr Thomas, nice to see you back again."

Sandra must be in her mid-forties. She looks as though she's had a tragic life but is bearing up bravely and doesn't want to talk about it, and for that I'm truly grateful.

"Have one yourself, Sandra."

"Bit early for me Mr Thomas, thanks all the same."

Was that a rebuke? Well who cares if it was.

Where was I? Ah yes, that's the Seventies done with. And so, without further ado we stumble bleary eyed and unshaven into the Eighties.

Julie was in the sixth form by then, and had discovered the

existence of Injustice. At first I assumed she'd turned into a raving Trot to annoy her mother, who'd embraced Thatcher and all her works with alarming enthusiasm.

"My God, Surrey's so *bourgeois*. You're regarded as a dangerous radical if you wash your car less than once a week."

On my access days, she'd badger me into driving her to Maerdy, so she could visit her Salt of the Earth Welsh grandparents. She'd sit cross-legged on the floor, head cocked to one side, as dad trotted out The People's History of Maerdy.

"Little Moscow, that's what they called this place in the Thirties."

How the men were always first out, last back in any strike; how they elected the first Communist mayor in the country.

"A woman too! Not much older than yourself."

Rolled out the story of him joining the International Brigade, and fighting in Spain. Meeting Paul Robeson.

"He came to the front to sing for the Republicans. They set up loudspeakers so we could all hear. When he started singing, both sides, us and the fascists, stopped fighting, and both sides applauded when he finished. I'll never forget it."

And, of course, how he came to the Rhondda a couple of years later to film *Proud Valley*.

"He could have had his pick of big money Hollywood films, but he chose to make a film about the working man here in the Rhondda. That's the kind of bloke he was, see."

I found it hard to conceal my boredom.

Afterwards, driving back down the M4, Julie said, "You're so lucky."

"Why do you say that?"

"It really *means* something to come from the Rhondda. What does it mean to come from Surrey? Nothing!"

Actually I thought it would be a relief to come from someplace where the huge weight of history wasn't always pressing down on you, trying to mould you into a familiar shape.

"Why didn't you give me a Welsh name?"

"What's wrong with Julie?"

Julie Christie was Miranda's heroine. Had been ever since that first appearance in *Billy Liar*, where she'd skipped down the streets of that bleak northern town, a free spirit, unaffected by her surroundings.

"It's so Sixties."

"You were *born* in the Sixties love."

"Don't call me love, it's patronising to women."

"Ah, I forgot."

We passed a battered Ford, covered in *Coal Not Dole* stickers. Julie sat up, waved frantically at the people inside; they waved back, beeped their horn.

"Dad! Go on, beep them back!"

"Oh, alright."

"It's great when you see other people on the same side, isn't it?"

"Uh-huh. You don't object when grandad calls you love."

She ignored this.

"Have you noticed how little my mother says? I mean, basically, when we visit them, it's to listen to one long monologue from grandad."

"Except you you always 'pop out' to the off licence and come back an hour later."

"I'd go mad without a break. To you those stories are fresh and exciting, all the things they never taught you about in school, to me it sounds like the needle's stuck."

"Gran always joins in the conversation when you've gone. You make her nervous."

"Me? How do I make her nervous?"

"Dad! You make *lots* of people nervous."

I burst out laughing. I couldn't believe what I was hearing.

"Like who?"

"Mummy, for one."

"Really?"

That cheeered me up. She certainly hid it well.

"People can't work out where you're coming from. They never know when you're being serious. They don't know where they are with you."

"Do *you* know?"

"No dad, I don't."

I was shocked by the hurt in her eyes. We fell into an uneasy silence. There were some services coming up.

"Fancy a coffee?"

Someone had left a tabloid on the table. The usual headline about violence on the picket lines.

"How can people believe this stuff?" she asked angrily.

She'd got up at 4.00 a.m. the previous week, bunked off school and went to picket a power station in Kent with a friend.

"When are *you* going to do something?"

"Me?"

"Yes, you. How can you not be affected by all this?"

"Who says I'm not affected?"

"You don't act like you are."

"What do you want me to do? Run up and down the street, waving a red flag?"

"You could do *something*."

"What?"

She rolled her eyes, pressed her index finger to her chin.

"Duh! Let's see now, what could you possibly do? Oh I know, how about fire-eating?"

She slapped the table in frustration.

"*Sing* of course. You could sing at benefits."

"Right, that'd give everyone a good laugh."

I reached for the paper, started flicking through it. After a few seconds, she slapped her hands down on the page I was looking at.

"You'd be great."

I couldn't fathom the look in her eyes. Was she thinking I *was* a good singer, or did she *want* me to be one?

"Don't you think I'm a bit old to join the class war?"

She squeezed my hand.

"Do it for me."

At my first benefit, I took a huge risk, deciding to sing *Joe Hill*, the way Robeson did, accompanied only by a piano player.

For those few minutes, while I was up on my hind legs, chest out, singing that old Socialist anthem I felt... what exactly? That it wasn't too late to turn back the tide, that if we stood together they'd never win, we could forge a new alliance between, oh, you know the kind of thing. I was good though. I *moved* them. It was, if I say so myself, the highlight of the show. The audience *expected* the other acts to be good.

I never knew the old bugger had it in him, did you?

I thought he was dead.

I was asked to record my version of *Joe Hill* for a compilation album, *Digging Deep for the Miners*. A strange record, consisting of folk songs, reggae tracks, jazz, an angry punk band backed by a male voice choir. I can't for the life of me think what kind of person might have bought it.

Julie, however, got very excited.

"This could be the start of something, dad. You're only as old as The Stones."

God knows where she got that kind of optimism.

Before long *The Sun* picked up on my change of direction. What fun they had.

Dafft Taff! He used to sing with Pinky and Perky, now he's serenading Scargill!!

Crispin was suitably droll.

"I hope this doesn't mean you're going to start singing *The Red Flag* at Butlins this summer."

He rushed me into the recording studio to cut my first single for nearly a decade. *My Hometown*, a bluesy ballad about a town ravaged by unemployment. It fell between two stools, too sentimental to appeal to a young audience, just a touch too modern to please my old fans.

Julie tried her best to sound enthusiastic.

"It's *great* dad. I love it."

She put its rapid appearance in the REDUCED rack down to a right-wing conspiracy to prevent airplay, bless her.

Time for a top up.

While she's serving me, Sandra starts asking about my touring schedule, family, holiday plans, in such a determinedly polite fashion that it's obvious she doesn't really like me. It's a relief for both of us when the transaction is over.

Ah, that's better.

So.

A few months after that abortive single, Julie and I were having lunch in my flat in London. The TV was on in the background. Another report about the increasing numbers of miners returning to work. It sent her into a rage.

"Lies! They're nothing but a mouthpiece for the government, Thatcher has got the BBC so frightened..."

"The strike's had it. It's only a matter of time."

Her knife and fork clattered to the table.

"Dad!"

"The Tories have been preparing for this for years. They'll bankrupt the country rather than give in now. It's hopeless."

"How can you say that?"

"Because I'm a lot older than you. Because I know how bad it feels to be on the losing side, and I'm preparing myself well in advance. You should too."

"No!"

She pushed her plate away.

"How can you say something like that? You sang that Paul Robeson song so beautifully, I can't believe you didn't mean every word."

I gave up on my meal, topped up our glasses.

"*I*, of course, actually met him."

She pulled a face.

"The Cardiff Capitol, 1958, I know. Grandad told me."

"I was left with a very different impression to your grandad."

"He said Paul Robeson was wonderful."

"Oh he was. Undoubtedly the greatest singer I ever saw, no question."

I leant back, took a drink of wine.

"All my life I'd dreamt of seeing the great Paul Robeson. But when we met him backstage, when I finally saw him close up, he frightened me."

"*Frightened* you?"

"In here," I pointed to my eyes, "I could see how lonely he was. All his talk about community and solidarity couldn't hide that. I'd heard so much about his tremendous charisma but, to me, the aura that surrounded him felt like a carefully constructed barrier, designed to keep people at a distance. It was as if he were directing himself in a one man show. It was a brilliant performance, but that's what it was, a performance."

"That's a horrible thing to say."

"Is it? Can you imagine the strain of carrying so many people's hopes for so long?"

She just stared at me, not wanting to hear any of this. But she couldn't look away, and I couldn't stop.

"On the train back home, grandad was estatic. 'The Yanks thought they could break him by confiscating his passport and stopping him from working, but they should have realised they'd never break a man like Robeson. It's all water off a duck's back to him.'"

"And how did he get his passport back? The campaign by workers in dozens of different countries. Solidarity won the day."

"And how did he end up? A broken man. A nervous break-down they reckon now, before spending his last years a total recluse. All those people like my father, who wouldn't let him just be a man, who demanded some kind of superhuman Soviet-style hero, they destroyed him just as much as the Yanks."

"No!"

"Yes. And it's a lesson for us all."

Julie was shaking her head, pushing her chair from the table, backing away.

"I can't believe you really think like that. I can't..."

She started crying. I got to my feet, called out after her.

"Julie!"

But she was already at the door.

Time for another, I think.

"Back again, Mr Thomas?"

"Please, it's Paul. A double. Have one yourself Sandra."

"Thanks, I'll have an orange juice."

"Go on, have a proper drink."

She smiles. Sorry but no. Sod her. I make my way back to my chair.

Whoops.

"Sorry mate."

The place is beginning to fill up now. What a bunch. They've got that pitiful, desperate look that says *Morecambe is the only place I feel at home anymore*. In the corner, a young lad in a white jacket and dickie bow has started playing the piano. Cocktail hour muzak, all part of the Midland's attempt to remind its users of its heyday in the Thirties. I get up, wander across.

"Hey mate, do you know *Joe Hill*?"

"Pardon me?"

Too young, far too young, what am I thinking of?

"Let me hum it for you."

He's looking round, an anxious expression on his face, I start without him.

"I dreamed I saw Joe Hill last night
Alive as you and me
But Joe, you're ten years dead I said,
I never died said he
I never died said he.

The copper bosses killed you Joe
They... they... the bosses they...

"bloody hell, don't just sit there gawping like a bunch of morons, somebody help me out!"

"Come on now, Mr Thomas, let's sit down, shall we?"

It's Sandra and some young kid in a suit. They take me gently by the elbows, guide me away from the piano.

"Do you like Paul Robeson, Sandra?"

"Yes, he's my favourite."

"*Really?* He was great though, wasn't he? How's *your* life, Sandra? Don't you find... where's this?"

"The manager's office, Mr Thomas. Here, sit down, drink this."

She pours me a mug of black coffee.

"What time does your show start tonight?"

I wave my arm at her.

"To hell with that."

I'm in one of those expensive leather recliners. I lean back, put my feet up on the desk.

"Here," she puts the mug in my hand.

"Thanks love."

The barmaids and waitresses and landladies I've had down the years. The married ones are the loneliest, I've always found.

"What time do you get off work Sandra?"

"Please don't Mr Thomas."

"Paul!"

"Paul. You just concentrate on sobering up, eh?"

"Pah! I could do that set in my sleep."

I take a swig of the coffee, reach inside my jacket for my wallet, pull out a photo.

"That's my daughter, Julie."

"She's lovely."

"Isn't she? She's out in Africa, being a do-gooder. I get a postcard from her about once a year."

"Kids eh?"

Suddenly I'm crying.

"I'm sorry."

"That's OK, you have a good cry love, you'll feel better for it."

We both know this is a lie.

I wipe my eyes, take another swig of coffee.

"I just need to check something, will you be alright here for a few minutes?"

"Yes, of course."

I look at my watch — two hours to go. There's no way I can face The Undead without another drink. I'll have to go to The Clarendon, no chance of getting served here now. I'll skip the soundcheck. It won't be the first time.

Hope I can manage "It's really great to be back in Morecambe" without choking on the words, or being struck down by a bolt of lightning.

A DAY OFF

A wind from Siberia roared down The Broadway. About fifty of us waited outside the Cricklewood Tavern, huddled together for warmth. There was a newsagent's further down, where you could shelter under the awning, but I'd always stood outside the Tavern, rain, hail or snow.

The first transit van pulled up at just gone six. I turned to Eamon, he was leaning against the wall, arms folded, eyes closed, yawning. I nudged him.

"Here they come, try and look a bit smart, for god's sake."

He swore under his breath, opened his eyes, and slowly pulled himself back to his full height. The ganger climbed out of the van, turned up his collar against the rain, began walking along the pavement in front of us, pointing to the ones he wanted.

"You.... You.... You."

I felt my heart thumping as he approached. He stopped in front of me, his eyes flicked over my arms and chest.

"...You."

I let out a breath; it was Eamon's turn next. He'd be alright if he managed to keep his eyes open, he had twenty years on me.

"...You."

"Begob you won't regret it, I'm a great man with the pick and shovel," said Eamon, putting on a thick Kerry accent and grinning like an eejit. The ganger stiffened.

"Are you taking the piss, son?"

"What do you mean?"

Eamon looked puzzled. The ganger hesitated, then suddenly jerked his thumb at the van.

"Go on, get in there before I change my mind."

I grabbed hold of Eamon and tugged him away before he could say anything else. When I'd promised my brother Tom

I'd look out for him when he came to London I never realised what I was taking on.

"Stop acting the gom, for Christ's sake."

He just laughed. He thought he was hilarious. We climbed into the back of the van. A big red-faced culchie squeezed up next to me.

"Hello," he said, "My name's Lonnegan" in a booming Kerry accent. He held out his hand till I shook it. I hoped to Jesus he hadn't heard Eamon putting on that voice.

"Terrible weather, you'd need to be an Eskimo to stick it," he said, blowing on his big paws, then rubbing them together. I nodded, and quickly looked away, the last thing I wanted at that time in the morning was to get stuck with a bore like him. The van filled up. Lonnegan turned to the fella sitting opposite.

"You'd need to be an Eskimo to stick this."

The man pretended not to hear him. As soon as the ganger closed the doors, everyone lit up. The smoke from the fags and the steam rising from our clothes formed a thick fog inside the van. The coughing started. One morning one of us will end up with a pair of lungs in a steaming heap on our lap.

Jesus! My lungs! How am I going to smoke now?

We joined the North Circular. The ganger put his foot down. Lonnegan was getting on everyone's nerves, whistling *The Merry Ploughboy* and tapping his feet. Eamon grabbed a rolled-up newspaper someone had left on the floor, started banging it on his knee and singing:

There she stood in the street,

"Jesus, put a sock in it, will you?" said Lonnegan. Eamon carried on singing, louder now, pretending the rolled up paper was a microphone.

Smiling from her head to her feet.

"For fuck's sake!" roared Lonnegan.

The ganger shouted over his shoulder.

"Shut up back there — you fecking Kerrymen are giving me a headache."

He turned the radio on. It was the weather forecast — wet and windy in the south, black ice in the north, Scotland completely fucked.

No matter, the Paddies are off to work.

*

Eamon said, "Wouldn't it be great if you were building your own house for a change?"

I grunted, and swung my pick. It was a right bastard of a morning, the icy rain was driving into us, the ground was as hard as rock.

"I'd have a conservatory, so you could catch the sun in the morning. Everything would be in white — the furniture, the carpets, the walls. And I'd have a spiral staircase coming down through the centre of the living room."

Lonnegan started snorting.

"I'd soundproof one of the rooms and turn it into a home recording studio."

"Jesus, you'd need soundproofing if you were going to be singing," said Lonnegan. A few of the others laughed.

Eamon stopped digging and leaned on his pick.

"In the garden," his eyes lit up as he waved his hand out in front of him, "a guitar shaped swimming pool."

"Will you listen to that fella?" said Lonnegan, turning to the others. "You don't want much, do you son? I suppose you think you're better than the rest of us?"

"No, just you."

Lonnegan's face turned even redder than it already was.

"You cheeky young whelp, I'll fecking..."

I jumped in between them.

"Ah now lads."

Lonnegan tried to push past me.

"Out of me way, this is nothing to do with you."

"He didn't mean any harm. You're sorry, aren't you Eamon?"

"Like fuck I am."

Lonnegan was strong as an ox, I couldn't have held him for long.

Luckily the others started giving out to him.

"Leave the cunt alone, willya?"

"Pack it in for Christ's sake, before you get us all the sack."

"No one talks to me like that," said Lonnegan, pointing over my shoulder at Eamon. "I'll see you after work. We'll see how cocky you are then."

Eamon tried to laugh it off but I could tell he was scared, Lonnegan would snap him like a twig. We went back to work.

No one said anything for a while, the only sounds were the odd grunt and the crunch of pickaxes cutting into the ground.

A few minutes later Eamon slammed his pick into a water pipe and a jet of water shot up into the air. He jumped back and started laughing. We all scrambled out of the trench apart from Eamon, who stood there in the rising water, holding his pick like one of those electric guitar yokes and singing.

Help me baby I'm drowning
Drowning in your love.

"Get out of there," I yelled. He took no notice. I jumped back into the trench and grabbed the pick.

"Come on, pack it in, for Christ's sake."

We wrestled the pick back and forth between us. The others stood above us, watching. We must have looked a right pair, him laughing like an eejit, me cursing him at the top of my voice.

The ganger pushed his way through the crowd.

"Right that's it. I knew you were trouble. Youse two are sacked."

He bunged us a few measly quid. Eamon started demanding more, but I pulled him away. When we were at a safe distance, Eamon turned around and yelled, "You can stick your job up your arse" at the ganger and flashed Lonnegan a V sign. As we walked past the portacabin, he picked up a stone and flung it at the window.

"Cut it out. What's come over you today?"

"Stop nagging, you're worse than my da."

We walked off the site. A rusting corrugated iron fence stretched down both sides of the road.

"Where are we?" asked Eamon.

"I've no idea."

"Ah, sweet Jesus."

I lit a couple of fags and passed him one, then checked my watch, it was nearly one.

"Right or left?" asked Eamon. There was a railway bridge a few hundred yards to our left, I remembered going under it in the van.

"Left."

The rain turned to hail, stinging our faces and hands, spraying the fence like buckshot, bouncing across the pavement.

Eamon grabbed me by the elbow, he had to shout to make himself heard above the din.

"The only thing for it is the high stool. Come on, I'm buying."

We ran like fuck.

The barmaid looked at us as if we were dirt under her fingernails. Our jeans were caked in mud, and it was streaked on our faces; Eamon's long hair was hanging in rat's tails. She poured our two pints in thirty seconds flat, you'd think she was turning on a water tap. We bought a couple of hot pies, our stomachs were howling, we hadn't had anything to eat since 5.30 that morning.

It was a dreary place, barely half full. I don't think anyone had smiled in there since it had opened. We found a table, as I bit into the pie the middle broke open, spilling half the meat and gravy onto the floor.

"Fuck it!"

Eamon roared laughing.

"Go on, laugh. Everything's a big joke to you, isn't it?"

He grinned, slowly took a bite out of his own pie, holding one hand carefully underneath it.

"You'd better buck up your ideas. You can't afford to carry on the way you did this morning in the building trade."

"Yes I can."

He looked delighted with himself.

"What do you mean?"

"I'm not going back to The Broadway."

He licked some gravy off his fingers.

"I've had enough. There's more to life than swinging a pick."

I could tell it was a line he'd been rehearsing for a long time.

"And what are you going to do instead?"

"Concentrate on my music."

He put down the pie, pulled a crumpled piece of paper from the back pocket of his jeans.

"I'm going to form a band. I've been working on an advert to go in the *NME*."

He unfolded the paper and read from it.

"Lead guitarist/singer/songwriter into Free, Led Zeppelin,

Deep Purple, Rory Gallagher etc. seeks bass player, drummer and keyboards to form progressive rock band. No ELP/Yes fans."

He gazed proudly at his handiwork for a few moments before folding the paper up again and slipping it back into his pocket. He took a sip of his pint.

"I'm not really sure about the keyboard player. I don't want to end up with some guy who thinks he's Keith Emerson or Rick Wakeman, you know? There's only going to be room for one soloist in my band."

"Concentrate on your music indeed. You'll be fecking lynched if you try and play that electric guitar in the boarding house again."

He paused, took a fag from his packet, tapped it on the table. He knew very well I was watching him, but he wouldn't meet my eye. When he spoke, he looked over towards the bar, as if something had caught his eye there.

"I'm moving into a squat in Notting Hill."

"A squat? What kind of people have you been hanging around with?"

He laughed to himself.

"A bunch of weirdos. They're going to take a vote on Wednesday to decide if I can move in."

"A vote?"

"Yeah, they do everything democratically. But it's a foregone conclusion. There's a couple of gorgeous birds there, they've fallen for my Celtic charm."

He laughed again, lit the fag. He offered me one, finally brave enough to look at me. I waved it away.

"Your Celtic charm? Jesus Christ, if you father was here now he'd give you a good kick up the arse."

He thought that was funny too.

"You know what really clinched it? When I played them a few jigs and reels on the mandolin. Jesus I had them eating out of my hand after that."

"I thought you were bored with all that?"

"So did I, till I found out how much those two liked the old diddley diddley."

"You watch you don't go and make a fool of yourself."

He rolled his eyes.

"Thanks for the advice."

He finished off the pie, then took a long swig of his pint.

"Jesus, that's better. I feel nearly human."

Suddenly he clapped his hands together.

"Let's see if we can wake the dead."

He got up and put some money in the juke box. Two beefy fellas carrying pints of lager came and sat at the next table. They started talking about football. Every second word was wanker. This one was a wanker, that one was a wanker. Eamon came back with two more pints.

"It was my shout."

He shook his head and put them down on the table.

"No, you're alright Uncle Sean."

He winked at me, raised his glass.

"To our day off."

He started singing along to the song on the juke box:

There she stood in the street,

Two more fellas joined the pair at the table opposite. I didn't like the look of them.

"Why the long face?"

"We've lost a day's wages, thanks to you."

"Don't worry, I'll treat you. I had a win on the horses at the weekend. All Right Now, a tenner at 7-1 in the 3.15 at Chepstow."

He tapped his nose.

"And another twenty on Wild Rover at 3-1 in the 4.00 at Doncaster."

He struck the table with the palm of his hand.

"The milky bars are on me!"

He laughed and took a swig from his pint.

"I see they caught the four Paddies who blew up that pub in Guildford," said one of the fellas at the next table in a loud voice.

"Yeah, the fucking animals," another replied. "Hanging's too good for them."

Nobody moved. It was as if somebody had knocked a glass off a table, and we were all waiting for it to shatter on the floor.

"Come on," I said, "drink up and let's go. This place is a dead loss."

"Aye you're right so," says Eamon. He finished the rest of

his pint in one and glanced over at the men sitting at the other table. They stared back at him.

"Come on if you're coming," I said, rising from my seat, careful not to catch their eye.

Rows of mean, grey, terraced houses stretched down the road. I imagined people peeking out at us from behind the net curtains, thinking *Look at those two filthy Paddies. What are they up to round here? I think I'll call the police.*

Flakes of snow tumbled from the grey sky. We walked on in silence. Tom would hit the roof when he heard Eamon was giving up work and moving into a squat. He'd blame me of course.

We came to a row of sad-looking shops. Old newspapers and carrier bags blew about in the wind, wrapping themselves around people's legs. Eamon bought whisky, beer and fags in a supermarket. There was a bus stop just outside. All the glass had been smashed, the wind whistled straight through, blowing flurries of snow into our faces. Big wet flakes settled on Eamon's hair and the tips of his eyelashes. We started drinking the whisky, trying to warm ourselves up. A police car crawled past, the coppers had a long, hard look at us. We stared at the ground till they'd gone. Eamon spat into the road.

"Feckers."

I said nothing.

"Do you think the buses actually stop here anymore?" Eamon asked, handing me the bottle. He turned his back to the wind, so he could light a couple of fags.

"I'd say we'll need a miracle."

I took a good swig from the bottle, wiped my mouth with the back of my hand.

"Perhaps we should say a few Haily Marys?"

He smiled and passed me the fag. I took a long drag; the smoke and booze were helping to keep the hunger at bay. I gave him back the bottle.

"I'm heading straight for the caff when we get back. I'm going to have lamb chops, roast spuds and peas, a mug of tea, apple crumble and custard."

Eamon gazed up into the sky, half closing his eyes.

"I'll have steak and kidney pie, chips, and beans, and bread and butter pudding after."

He pulled a sour face.

"They're all vegetarians in the squat. You ought to have seen what we had the other night — Fennel Casserole. Jesus, it was like chewing on cardboard. That stuff wouldn't fill a rabbit. As soon as I left I ran round to the nearest kebab house and got myself a doner and chips."

He raised the bottle to take another swig, then turned and looked at me; we roared laughing.

I heard a muffled rumbling noise.

"Listen."

It was a bus, struggling stubbornly through the driving snow, like an old tub pitching and rolling in a heavy sea. Eamon jumped to his feet and threw his arms around me, laughing like a maniac.

"It's a miracle Uncle Sean."

"Get off me you big eejit."

I stepped into the road and stuck out my hand.

We sat upstairs, on the back seat. It stank of stale smoke and damp clothes; cigarette butts littered the floor. There were a handful of other passengers dotted around. They looked like corpses someone had propped up in the seats in a desperate effort to make the bus look full. The only sign of life was a woman downstairs, humming a merry tune.

We passed a burnt-out corner shop, Ali's Stores; a car dumped in a canal, the roof already covered in snow. I still had no idea where we were.

"London is a huge place," said Eamon, "I don't think you'd ever get to know all of it, even if you lived here your whole life."

"There's a lot of it you'd be better off not knowing."

"Did you never think of going back home, Uncle Sean?"

"Sure there's nothing there for me to go back for."

"Weren't you and Geraldine Cullen going together once?"

I nodded and took the whisky bottle from him, it was half empty already.

"My da thought you'd get married."

"So did I. Once I'd made enough money here I was going to go back and propose to her."

"What happened?"

"I'd been in London less than a year when your father wrote and warned me to come home as soon as I could, that Gerry Cullen was after her, but I took no notice. I was sure she'd wait."

Neither of us said anything for a minute. He passed me the whisky. I took a good shot of it.

"The Cullens have always had plenty of money. None of them ever needed to leave home."

"Money's not everything."

"That's just something poor people tell themselves."

I looked out of the window. An old woman hauling a shopping trolley went on her arse in the snow. A couple of teenagers laughed at her. I took another couple of hefty swigs of the whisky then passed the bottle back to Eamon. He started singing that awful song again:

There she stood in the street

I nudged him.

"Sing *The Cliffs of Dooneen*."

He sighed.

"Alright, just this once when no one I know is looking, alright?"

He started to sing:

You may travel far far from your native home,
Far away o'er the mountains far away o'er the foam,
But of all the fine places that I've ever been,
There is none can compare with the cliffs of Dooneen.

I'd always loved that song. Someone told me that it's about Dooneen Point, near Ballybunion in County Kerry. I've never been there, but I could tell you exactly what it looks like.

Someone started coming up the stairs, humming, money jingling with every step. The conductress, a black woman about my own age, appeared. It was a bastard of a day but she wasn't going to let that stop her from enjoying herself. She was a sight for sore eyes. She smiled at Eamon. It was a beautiful smile.

"Now there's a happy customer. Singing away."

She was the first person that day we hadn't made angry or

nervous.

"Do you like it? It's about a place in County Kerry called the Cliffs of Dooneen. Have you ever been there?"

She pulled a sad face, as if she was going to cry.

"Never."

She put her hand on her hip and raised her eyebrows.

"And I suppose now you're going to tell me exactly what I've been missing."

She was a gas, she should have been on the television.

"It's a beautiful place on a fine summer's day, the wildflowers out, the mountains behind you, the clear blue sea in front of you. You'd love it."

She laughed.

"You gonna take me there honey?"

"Would you come?"

"Now what would they think of someone like me in a place like that?"

"Sure they'd love you. You'd be treated like a film star."

"Well now, that's tempting. It's about time somebody treated me like a film star."

Eamon laughed.

"Ah you're a star alright love, don't you worry."

"So you'll come?"

"It's the best offer I've had all day. I promise to think about it."

"Where does this bus go anyhow?" Eamon asked.

"Where d'you want to go?"

"Kilburn."

She scratched the back of her neck with her finger.

"Well now, we're a good way from there, but I'll tell you where you can pick up a Number 8."

We bought our tickets. Eamon asked her to have a drink with us.

"I'd love to darling, but I'm not allowed when I'm on duty."

"Ah go on."

"If an inspector got on and saw me drinking I'd be in big trouble and this is the only job I got y'know."

"I'll bet it's a hard job and all," I said.

"You're not kidding. I been on my feet since six this morning."

The bell rang then and she went back downstairs, humming to herself. Eamon handed me the bottle again, it was nearly empty. The whisky had warmed me up nicely. Suddenly the day felt full of promise. I started wondering what the others in the house would say if I ever brought back a black woman. Their mouths would fall open. They wouldn't know where to look. It'd be a good one alright. All of a sudden I had a mind to do it, just for the craic. I listened to her humming to herself downstairs, I tried to pick out the tune, but I didn't know it. I wondered if anyone had ever tried to work out how many different tunes there were in this world? It'd make your head spin just thinking about it.

She shouted up the stairs at us.

"All those wanting Kilburn, change at the next stop."

It seemed hardly any time had passed since we'd got on.

"Let's stay on for a while," I said to Eamon.

He looked at me as if I'd gone mad.

"What for? Christ we don't even know where the bloody bus is going."

It was a stupid thing to say.

"Come on, will you?"

He pushed against me, I got up out of the seat and started walking downstairs.

She was standing on the platform, smiling.

"Bye now love," said Eamon, and stepped off.

I stopped in front of her, swaying slightly, trying to think of something to say. She moved back a step.

"Are you alright?" she said, frowning.

"Come on!" shouted Eamon from the pavement. "There's a Number 8 coming."

I wanted to say something that would make her smile again. My tongue swelled up in my mouth.

"Come on!"

"You'd better hurry or you'll miss your bus," she said. She sounded worried, as if she was afraid I wouldn't go. The passengers were staring at me. I lowered my face and stepped off the platform. The Number 8 drew up. We sat upstairs again. Eamon passed me a beer. I tilted back my head and drank it in one.

"Sing *The Cliffs Of Dooneen* again," I said to Eamon.

"Ah give it a rest, will you?"

He leaned his head against the window and closed his eyes.

I reached inside the carrier bag for another beer, drank it staring into the driving snow. It's going to be a bad morning on The Broadway tomorrow.

LIFE ON THE RESERVATION

The view from up there was brilliant. The town was on our right, to our left the countryside — the forest, the valley, the river turning gold in the sun. Red Cloud took out his tin of tobacco and started rolling a cigarette, I peeled another stick of gum. Wood smoke drifted through the trees from the camp below.

"It's good to get away from the reservation, isn't it?" said Red Cloud.

"Yes, it is."

I lay down on the grass, felt the sun warming my face.

"At least you have this beautiful countryside on your doorstep," he said. "The reservation where I grew up was a huge place, nothing but mile after mile of ugly concrete."

"Where did you grow up, Red Cloud?"

He sighed and took a long drag from his cigarette before answering.

"Cardiff. I lived there for many years before I even realised I was an Indian, the white man's bad medicine had affected me so much."

A lamp post on the edge of the estate began to flicker into life. Some of them came on in the afternoon and went off again at night, others buzzed all day and night like angry wasps without ever lighting up.

Red Cloud raised his face to the sky, squinting in the sun as he spoke.

"To be happy and healthy you need fresh air, sunshine and open spaces. When I was a young man I left the reservation and for the last thirty years I have wandered where I pleased. If the Great Spirit wanted us to stay in one place He would make the world stop moving. You must leave the reservation when you grow up, my son."

He shook his head.

"It is not a natural life. If you stay there you will go crazy."

Dad was recording the hoover.

"How much longer for god's sake?" shouted mam. She was holding Helen, she'd done a big dribble down her blouse.

Dad frowned, took out his ear plugs.

"What?"

"How much longer?" she shouted again, "I'm getting a headache."

He bent down to check how much space was left on the cassette.

"About another twenty minutes I reckon."

He looked delighted with himself.

"This'll teach that bastard next door."

Lyndon ran into the room, flapping his cloak and humming the Batman theme.

"Stop that!" shrieked mam, "We're going to your nan's soon, you'd better behave or else."

After dad had finished making the tape he was going to set the music centre to come on at six in the morning, but we'd get a good night's sleep at our nan's. We had noisy neighbours on both sides; Barry was always playing his music too loud, and the Harnetts' dog, Buster, never stopped barking.

"You realise this is only going to make things worse, don't you?"

Dad stretched back in the chair, put his hands behind his head. He didn't say anything. He had that look on his face, the one that made her lose her patience.

"I wonder about you sometimes Alan, I really do."

It is not a natural life on the reservation, if you stay there you will go crazy.

Dad's face went tight.

"Would it be too much to ask you to back me up just once instead of criticising everything I do?"

They stared at each other. I held my breath. If one of them spoke now, there'd be a row. I prayed to the Great Spirit to keep the peace. Mam scowled, turned away and walked out of the room. Helen was dribbling down her back now, Dad put his earplugs back in, and carried on reading the paper. It had worked, the Great Spirit had heeded my prayers.

*

"Is your dad in?"

It was Barry.

When dad went to the door, Barry said "Funny bastard, aren't you?"

"I beg your pardon?"

"Try laughing this off."

Dad staggered back, holding his face. He knocked over the little table with the telephone on it and collapsed on the floor. Mam came running out of the living room.

"Oh god, what now?"

There was a crash from the other side of the door, Helen started bawling, Buster started barking.

"Barry hit him."

She rolled her eyes.

"Are you happy now? I told you. I warned you."

He swore at her through his hands. She went back inside to see what was the matter with Helen. Dad started shouting at me.

"What did you tell him I was in for?"

In ancient times, we went where we pleased. We felt close to nature, the Earth was our mother, animals, plants and birds were children of the Earth, and treated with respect. Hunters said a prayer to an animal before they killed it.

"Forgive me my brother, but my people must eat."

Then the white man came, discovered coal on our ancestral hunting grounds, took them from us and forced us to live on reservations while they tore up the earth. Our old way of life disappeared. Our spirit died.

I knelt on his chest, held him down with one hand, started pulling off his mask with the other. It had been easy to get him on the ground, he was wearing roller skates; I pushed him, he fell, before he knew it I was on him.

"NO! NO! NO!"

He screamed, thrashing his arms and legs about, it was difficult to control him. I couldn't get the mask over his head, he was shaking it from side to side, making a weird whimpering noise.

I punched him again.

"I warned you."

I could hear the worry in my voice. He was turning scarlet, sobbing, gasping; he was starting to get hysterical. It wasn't going as I planned. I was frightened he'd choke. He began banging the back of his head against the ground.

"Alright!"

I got off him. Still he wouldn't stop.

"Alright, alright, keep it on."

I was angry, but scared now too. I looked around. I was safe for the moment, no one could see us, I'd dragged him into some bushes to get him.

What if he cracked his head open?

"Stop it!"

He wouldn't. He'd kill himself, I'd get the blame, I was older, he was only five.

"You're his brother, you were supposed to take care of him."

That's what they'd say.

"I'm going now, alright? You can stop. Keep your stupid mask on, do you hear me? Lyndon? Lyndon?"

I started walking away. I pushed through the bushes, picked up my bike. I wasn't going to look back, I was late already, Red Cloud would be wondering where I was. I looked back. He was still banging his head, he'd gone mad. It was his own fault, he'd tried to follow me, I kept warning him to go back home but he wouldn't take any notice.

"Where are you going?"

"Go back."

"Where are you going?"

"Go back I said."

There was no way I could take him with me, he'd spoil everything, he'd blab to mam and dad about the camp and they'd stop me from going there. It was my secret, it was nothing to do with him, or them.

He was going to knock himself out.

I threw the bike down, ran back, picked him up, shook him.

"Stop! Stop it will you?"

I held him close; I was crying.

"There there, there there."

I rocked him back and forth, just the way I'd seen mam do

it. He closed his eyes. Tears and snot trickled down my hand. I should never have tried to take his mask off. He wore his Batman outfit every day, even to school. Mam and dad had given up trying to make him wear anything else. There was a lump forming on the back of his head. He was my brother. He was crazy. It wasn't his fault, living on the reservation had done it.

The settlers kept digging more mines, building more factories and laying tracks for the Iron Horse on land that belonged to us for thousands of years. We were so few, they were so many, how could we resist them?

We sat in Red Cloud's tepee.

"I've seen the effect of opencast mining at Ffos Las, East Merthyr, Glynheath, Abercanaid. The walls of the houses shaking and cracking from the explosions, the coaldust blackening everything for miles around. No peace day or night. Your life will be hell if they start here."

"Tea?" said Pretty Hawk, Red Cloud's wife, passing the mugs. She took a blue one, gave me a red one, Red Cloud's had *CARDIFF CITY F.C. — THE BLUEBIRDS* written on the side. When he saw me looking at it, he smiled and held it up.

"I keep it to remind myself what my life used to be like when I was a white man. I worked in a factory, stacking boxes. All I dreamt about was football. I wanted to play for City, I was certain I was going to be the new John Charles — 'The Gentle Giant.'"

That would be a good name for Red Cloud.

"But I fell akwardly after making a tackle and ruptured my knee ligaments. That was the end of my football career."

"My ambition," said Pretty Hawk, "was to look like Dusty Springfield. To walk down the street and make people stop in their tracks, nudge their mates and say — 'Hey, isn't that Dusty?' I couldn't think of anything I wanted more."

I didn't know who she was talking about.

"A pop star. Before your time. Jaffa cake?"

"Yes please."

I dipped it into my tea, just long enough for it to turn really soggy without collapsing. It was a very difficult skill to master.

When Lyndon tried to copy me, his always collapsed into the mug.

"What do your parents think of what they plan to do here?" asked Pretty Hawk.

I shrugged. I didn't know, I'd never heard them talking about it. All they ever did was argue. You couldn't ask dad anything, he'd only make fun of you.

"Do you think we'll succeed in stopping them?" asked Red Cloud.

I didn't know. I wanted them to. I wasn't sure.

"Come, say what's on your mind."

"My dad says you can protest all you like but the bloody so and sos will go ahead and do what they want in the end like they always do, so you're wasting your time."

Red Cloud sipped his tea, nodded slowly to himself.

"The white man has stolen his heart."

I didn't know what to say. I felt ashamed.

He was right.

We were in the shopping centre. In the middle, under the glass ceiling was a jungle. It wasn't a real one, the trees, plants and grass were plastic. The grass was full of empty lager cans, crisp packets and chips. Dad started laughing. He walked up to the jungle, ducking down, peering through the trees, pretending to look for someone hiding inside there; he started shouting.

"You can come out now Mr Yashimoto, the war's over. There's a job waiting for you in South Wales, we need a new manager at the Sunrise Electronics factory."

That's where dad worked. Some people walking past laughed.

"Come on Alan," said mam, "People are looking."

"Let them look."

He'd been drinking. He started humming along to the piped music, *We'll Keep a Welcome in the Hillsides*, pretending to conduct the choir.

"Come on, don't be shy, we're all friends now."

Mam started walking away.

"I've had enough of your nonsense, come on Kevin, let's get the mince."

Dad climbed over the little wall, leaned against one of the

trees and lit a cigarette.

"You'll love it here. The house prices are very low. The people are friendly. Do you like golf?"

He threw back his head and blew out a cloud of smoke, then started giggling.

"No one ever mentions the war."

A woman walked past, eating a bag of chips. Her little girl skipped along in front of her, waving a huge chip and humming to herself. Her mouth dropped open when she saw dad.

"Mam, there's a man in the jungle."

"Don't be silly Angharad, eat your chip."

"Come on, there's nothing to be nervous about, there aren't any unions, we're very flexible these days we are. We never go on strike anymore, you can do what the bloody hell you like. They've just made fifty of us redundant, what did we do? Nothing. Absolutely nothing. Yeah, surplus to requirements, that's me."

"Alan!"

Mam was staring at him now. He stared back.

"You heard me. I've been given the chop."

He moved his hand through the air like a blade.

"Banzai!" he shouted, and burst out laughing; it turned into a coughing fit. Some people started pointing at him and laughing. I turned away.

It was an absolutely brilliant idea. It took all day. First I helped Red Cloud and Pretty Hawk dig the pits, then mix the cement. He filled the pits with concrete, then fixed an iron bar into each one. Some of the people who lived in the treehouses had gathered round to watch by then, wondering what we were doing.

"When I see them coming, I'll jump in here and handcuff myself to that bar," said Red Cloud, "and Pretty Hawk will do the same in there."

Pretty Hawk smiled at everyone. She was a lot older than Mam, but she looked really nice.

"They daren't try and cut through it, there's not enough room in there to swing a cat, they'd end up chopping my arm off. They'll have to dig around behind the concrete. When I did this in Crynant, it took them three days to get me out."

"Nice one," said Mole. He and Ratty had been digging tunnels all day, he was still wearing his miner's helmet with the floppy ears on the side. They had enough food and drink down there to last them for weeks.

Everyone helped each other out here, no one argued. On the reservation, they didn't know how to do anything except argue all day and get drunk down the pub. But here, everyone stuck together. The white man would never win.

Dad sat at home all day, drinking and watching TV. He never stopped complaining; everyone on it annoyed him.

"Not this moron again."

"How many times have they shown this now?"

"Bloody crap, I could have done better myself."

He never turned it off though. The white man's rubbish was rotting his brain. When the adverts were on, he turned the sound down and read his book, *Banzai You Bastards!*, about the way the Japanese tortured people during the war.

Him and mam hardly talked to each other at all now. If one of them came in the room, the other one would leave. Lyndon was too young to realise what was going on. Helen was just a baby. I was the only one who could do anything about it.

I tried talking to Mam first, she'd listen, Dad never listened.

"Go away, I'm busy."

She wasn't busy, she was standing on the back doorstep, smoking. She'd been crying.

"Mam, what's wrong?"

"Nothing, go and play."

I stayed where I was. I wanted to show her I understood, that I could see what was going on. That there was no need to pretend with me the way she did with Lyndon.

"You've no idea how much I've got on my plate."

She was always going on about how much she had on her plate. It didn't make any sense.

"We'll never be happy, trying to live like white people."

She lost her temper.

"For god's sake Kevin. Why can't you be like other kids?"

I didn't expect that.

"I don't know what you're on about half the time, I really don't. God knows where you get it from."

Her bottom lip started to tremble. She rubbed her forehead

with the tips of her fingers.

"You make me nervous, the way you hang around, watching me all the time. I don't know what you want from me. Why do you always have to look so bloody disapproving?"

"Mam, we have to leave the reservation..."

She frowned, screwed her eyes shut.

"What are you on about now? God, is there nowhere in this house I can get any peace?"

It was going wrong. This wasn't how I'd imagined it.

"Stop that!"

I was kicking the door jamb. I couldn't help it. She was making me nervous. As soon as she told me to stop it, I started kicking it even harder. I didn't mean to.

"Between you and your father I'll end up in St Woolos."

St Woolos was the mental home out on the edge of town. Mam said it was where they put people who couldn't cope. Dad said it was full of men who'd been driven mad by their wives.

"It couldn't be any worse than this."

She went and locked herself in the bathroom.

I was the only one who could see what was happening.

Once our lands stretched far to the east, all the way to the sea. But gradually the settlers pushed us back. We'd lost our colouring, become pale and weak, through being penned in for so long on the reservation. In our dreams, we were brave warriors but when we woke, or sobered up, we wept at what we'd become.

One minute it was a sunny afternoon, the next the streets were filling with thick black smoke. I ran inside, choking. A pounding noise started.

Thok! Thok! Thok!

The ground shuddered, the walls began to crack. Outside people were screaming. Helen started bawling, mam picked her up, clutched her to her chest.

"Oh god, what now?"

Dad was sat in front of the telly, drinking beer.

"There's something wrong with the reception."

"Where's Lyndon?" shouted mam, looking round frantically.

Dad got up out of his seat, started slapping the top of the telly with his hand.

"Bastard thing!"

The windows shattered, plaster showered down from the ceiling. Dad brushed the dust from his hair and shoulders, dragged his chair closer, leaned over and started shaking the telly.

"Come on. Don't give up on me now, I've got a fiver each way on the favourite in this one."

"Alan! Leave that. Help me find Lyndon."

The ground began to split open; there was a horrible scream as mam and Helen disappeared down a crack. The floor gave way beneath me, I plummeted downwards. At the last moment I managed to grab hold of one the legs of dad's chair.

"Dad! Help me!"

He was still shaking the telly.

"Come on Mr Ed, atta boy, you can do it!"

I couldn't hold on any longer.

I woke up with a start, covered in sweat. It was pitch black.

Thok! Thok! Thok!

I could still hear the pounding noise. I stretched out my hand and touched the wall — it was still solid. I turned over and checked the clock — ten-to-three.

Thok! Thok! Thok!

It was coming from the other side of the room. I switched on the light. Lyndon knelt on the bed, banging his head against the wall. Dad had nailed a cot mattress above his bed to make sure he didn't hurt himself when he started doing it. It would work fine for a while, then, even though he was fast asleep, Lyndon would shift position and start headbutting the bare wall again; he must have had some kind of radar.

Thok! Thok! Thok!

The doctor said it was very dangerous to try and wake him up when he was doing it, he might go crazy.

Thok! Thok! Thok!

I couldn't stand it any longer. All the doors and windows were wide open it was so hot. I got out of bed, went into mam and dad's room. Helen was curled up in a ball in one corner of her cot, the sheet twisted around her, one leg twitching. Mam was tossing and turning in the bed, muttering.

"Come back, come back here."

She was having her nightmare again, the one where me, Lyndon and Helen were tiny, no bigger than mice, and a rainstorm washed us off the pavement into the gutter and down the drain before she could do anything.

Outside in the street, the lampost was fizzing and crackling like a firework about to go off.

"Quick, get them out of there Alan."

She stretched her hand to the other side of the empty bed.

Thok! Thok! Thok!

I went downstairs. Dad had fallen asleep in front of the telly. He'd been watching sumo wrestling, he thought it was hilarious, said it reminded him of the Harnetts having an argument. There was a half empty bottle of whisky in his lap, empty cans of lager on the floor.

"Dad! Dad! It's Lyndon, get up will you?"

I shook his legs and arms.

"Help me!"

His head rolled to one side.

"Wake up!"

I was beating his arms and legs with my fists, getting angrier and angrier. It was useless, nothing would wake him. I grabbed the bottle, poured the rest of the whisky over his head, watched it run down his hair and cheeks, watched his mouth open greedily when it touched his lips. I knew he couldn't help it, I knew life on the reservation was making him crazy, but I hated him just the same.

Red Cloud sat cross legged on one of the flat rocks by the river, his hands folded in his lap, staring into the water. I sat next to him. It was so quiet and peaceful there. Neither of us had spoken for a long time. I couldn't imagine Red Cloud getting drunk every day like dad, he was always so gentle and calm. He raised his head, breathed out.

"I have just seen someone I have not seen for a long time."

I didn't understand.

"She visited me, in my memory."

He closed his eyes.

"A little girl. She held an apple in her hand."

Suddenly he looked very tired, and a lot older than dad. He

got to his feet.

"Come with me."

We walked over to a tree. Red Cloud grabbed the trunk, signalled for me to do the same on the other side.

"Listen," he said, pressing his ear to the bark. I did the same.

"Do you hear anything?"

I nodded. I didn't really.

"That is the sound of the Great Spirit passing through the tree."

I strained harder; I thought I heard it this time, just. A humming sound.

"The Great Spirit is all around us, in everything we see and touch. It is good. Remember that when you see bad things — do not despair, there is much good in this world. When I was a young man, I saw something so terrible I thought I would never recover. But then I discovered The Great Spirit, and was saved."

"What did you see, Red Cloud?"

He shook his head.

"I will tell you another time."

There was a drawing of a grinning brat standing beside a burning house on the front. It said HOMEWRECKER in large letters underneath, the kind of thing a little kid half Lyndon's age would wear. She turned to me.

"How about this? Do you think this would fit Kevin?"

"Mam, *I'm* Kevin."

She stared at me for a moment, frowning, then turned away. She put the tee shirt back on the rail where she found it, between the Teletubbies tee shirt and the tartan skirt.

"I can't do this anymore."

It was like she was talking to someone no one else could see. Helen was twisting and turning her head around in her push chair to see what was happening. Lyndon was hiding in a row of jackets. The other people in the shop were staring at us.

"Mam..."

Her eyes turned steely, she started shouting.

"Go on, take a good look. Feel better now you've found someone to look down on, have you?"

Helen started crying.

"Come on."

Mam set off too quickly, not looking where she was going, ran the pushchair over an old lady's foot. Lyndon panicked, ran straight into another lady, winding her. The lady behind the counter shouted at him.

"Watch where you're going, you little so and so."

We raced through the door, back out into the street. Lyndon got his cloak caught in the door and started squealing. I had to run back and hold it open so he could escape. As soon as we were a safe distance from the shop mam put her hand on her chest, closed her eyes.

"Mam, are you alright?"

She shook her head, gasping for breath.

"What's the matter?"

She motioned for me to take the pushchair. Helen was howling at the top of her voice, her face red as a berry. Mam bent her head, put her other hand against the wall to steady herself. Tears ran down her cheeks.

"I don't want to end up in St Woolos like my mother."

One man had passed out on the pavement outside the pub, another was throwing up in the gutter.

"It's Trevor and Wyn," said Dad. "I was planning to meet up with them today. Looks like they had a good time and all. Here I am, off to the bloody supermarket instead."

A man dressed up as Denzil the Dragon wandered round the shopping centre, handing out balloons and baseball caps with "I Love Opencast Mining" written on them. A couple of ladies wearing mini skirts and miners' helmets gave out leaflets.

"You could win a holiday in the sun..." said a man in a suit, speaking into a microphone. He wore a miner's helmet too.

"Just answer a few simple questions about open cast mining, complete our slogan and you could be heading for a two week holiday in sunny Spain."

Some kids started pulling Denzil's tail. He tried to kick them and nearly fell over; they laughed and ran off.

Lo Cost was packed, Dad nearly got into a fight with another man when their trolleys collided.

"Look where you're going, can't you?"

"What do you think you're doing, reversing round the corner at that speed you maniac?"

He'd just spotted a special offer on lager.

At the check out the man in front of us only had a bag of cheese and onion crisps in his basket, but as he reached over to pay, his jacket fell open and a couple of bottles of whisky fell out and smashed on the floor. Two security guards ran over, they closed the till and we had to join the back of another queue. By the time we'd finished dad was in a terrible mood. He headed straight for the little wall that surrounded the jungle, sat down and lit a fag.

"What a madhouse, I'm not looking forward to this every week, are you?"

"Every week?"

"If I've got to do it, you're bloody well coming with me."

There was a rustling noise behind us. We looked round, it was Denzil the Dragon, creeping around inside the jungle. He stopped a few feet away, looked behind him, then reached up and took his head off. He ran his hand over his red face, rubbed his eyes, muttering to himself.

"Fucking kids."

"Huw!" Dad shouted.

"Christ almighty, you nearly gave me a heart attack man."

"What the bloody hell are you doing?

"I snuck in here for a fag, gasping I am."

"You know what I mean."

They stared at each other for a few seconds, not saying anything.

"Christ, look at you."

Huw's face crumpled.

"You won't tell anyone?"

Dad shook his head.

"Come on man, have a drink. Kevin, get those cans of lager out."

Huw crouched down, edged towards where we sat, took up position behind a tree.

"Come out of there."

"I can't, if someone sees me I'll get the sack."

Dad rolled his eyes. Huw reached inside his costume and brought out his fags. I found the lager, dad took one himself, passed another to Huw.

"Cheers."

He swigged from the can.

"Christ, it's a bit rough, this."

"Special offer," said dad, "Four for £1.99."

Huw frowned, held the can up, looked at the bottom.

"They're past their sell-by date."

"Only just."

Huw sighed, took a drag from his fag, blew a long stream of smoke through his nose.

"This your eldest?"

Dad nodded, "Yeah."

"He looks just like you."

I didn't.

"What do you want to be when you grow up? Scrum half for Wales, eh?"

"An Indian warrior."

They gave each other a look I wasn't supposed to notice.

"Have you heard the rest of the staff at Sunset Industries have been put on a three-day week?"

"Yeah, I'll give it a couple of months at most before those bastards cut their losses and find somewhere else where they can pay the workers even less — like the Philippines."

A little girl stopped in front of us. She was eating a bag of chips, staring at Dad and Huw.

"Mam, there's a man dressed as a dragon sitting in the jungle, drinking beer."

Her mother rushed over, grabbed her by the arm, dragged her away so quickly her chips flew across the floor. She started crying.

"It serves you right, what have I told you about making things up?"

Dad threw back his head, polished off the can in one go. He screwed up his eyes, belched, chucked the can behind him into the jungle. He looked around him.

"How can you stand wandering round in here all day, dressed up in that stupid costume?"

"It's better than sitting at home on my own."

Dad gave him a quizzical look. Huw sighed, closed his eyes.

"Christine's left me for another bloke, taken the kids with

her."

"Who?"

"Greasy Joe."

That was what everybody called the bloke who owns the burger van that's always parked in the town centre.

"Promised to take her somewhere more glamorous."

"Where?"

"Apparently he's got relatives in Swindon."

Dad shook his head.

"Bugger me."

Huw took a long swig from his can, dad opened a new one.

"You're better off on your own mate. Look at me, Debbie's drugged up to the eyeballs. Me and Kevin got to do all the shopping now, she can't leave the house without having a panic attack."

Huw chucked his butt at a tree.

"It's a laugh, innit? She can't leave the house without cracking up, I can't bear to stay inside mine."

Dad stared at the floor.

"Yeah, it's bloody hilarious."

They'd never seen anything like it on the estate before. Dozens of kids ran along beside us, their hands over their mouths, whooping like the Indians on the telly. A group of men stood in a pub doorway, laughing and jeering.

"Fucking hell it's Tonto."

A pickled egg flew through the air, narrowly missing Red Cloud's head. He took no notice. He looked straight ahead, walking with his head held high, his chest out. We came to our road. As soon as we turned the corner, I heard the barking.

"That's him," I said, pointing at Buster, who was going round in circles in front of the Harnett's house as we approached. Red Cloud nodded.

"The four leggeds are our brothers. They are sacred too, and should be treated as such."

Mr Harnett had never let Buster back inside the house since he'd chewed up his *100 Greatest Goals Ever!* video when he was a puppy. The Harnetts chucked food through the window at him — left over boil-in-the-bag curries, wrinkled chips, stale bread. Buster bit anyone who came too close. Postmen wouldn't deliver letters anymore, the bin men refused to empty their bins — the stink was horrible.

People came out of their doorways to gawp at Red Cloud as he walked down our road. When Buster saw the crowd coming towards him, he ran in tighter, faster circles, his barking became more frantic. Red Cloud approached slowly, on his own now, the rest of us standing back, watching. Dad opened the door, his eyes were bleary, his hair stood on end.

"What the bloody hell's going on?"

When everyone ignored him, he followed their gaze till he saw Red Cloud walking slowly towards Buster, looking him straight in the eye. Dad blew out his cheeks, shoved his hands in his pockets.

"Christ almighty! It's life, Jim, but not as we know it."

Buster started growling. No one was laughing now.

I was scared.

Dad said, "Hey! watch it mate, he'll go for you."

Buster came to a halt, bared his teeth; the hair on the back of his neck stood up. It was what he looked like before he went for the postman. Red Cloud stretched out his hands in front of him, began chanting in a low voice. I became aware of another sound growing behind me, so low, coming from so far away that I could barely hear it, it was more like feeling something prickling the hairs on my skin than a sound. It grew louder, became a wind, roaring in my ears like the sea, blowing through the reservation, chasing away the fear. I felt it, everybody there felt it coming. The Great Spirit. Red Cloud knelt down, Buster went quiet; he didn't know what to do, didn't understand what was happening, he was used to everyone being frightened of him. There was a gasp from the crowd as Red Cloud placed his hands on Buster's head. His chanting became faster, louder.

I looked at Dad, standing on the doorstep, his mouth hanging open. The Harnetts were watching through their window, stuffing crisps into their mouths.

Red Cloud removed his hands, Buster sank to the ground, licked his lips and went to sleep. Red Cloud stood up.

"Respect all four-legged creatures my brothers and sisters. Respect yourselves also."

He looked around him.

"This is no way to live. If you stay here, you will grow sick and die."
The crowd parted to let him through.

Barry was away for the weekend; there was no noise from next door. Buster lay quietly on the grass outside the Harnett's house. Dad had been pacing up and down the living room all afternoon. Suddenly he stopped, put his head in his hands.
"I can't stand it. I can't stand this bloody silence."

We were given different water to the white man, special Reservation water filled with drugs that made us forget what great warriors we once were and how we could take back our lands and drive the settlers to the sea if we recovered our memories. Red Cloud told me this. And they fixed the news so that we never saw pictures of the white men poking fun at us in their big, expensive houses, pointing and laughing at our small, sad homes. If you tried to explain these things to other people on the reservation, they laughed.

"You've got to hand it to them," said Mr Harnett, "I mean I couldn't live up a tree, could you?"
"And just look what the Chief did for Buster," said Mrs Harnett.
That was what she called Red Cloud. Buster stretched out on the grass in front of us, quiet and still; a postman walked past and he didn't even blink.
"We're an indigenous people, we are," said Mrs Harnett, crossing her arms in front of her chest.
"That's right," said Mr Harnett, "and it's about time indigenous peoples had a say about what happens to their land. It's about time somebody listened to us, we're as good as anyone else."
Mr Harnett took a scrap of paper out of his back pocket, and started reading from it.
"'You said you wanted to put us on a reservation, to build us houses and make us medicine lodges. I was born where there were no enclosures and everything drew a free breath. I want to die there and not within walls.'"
Dad's mouth fell open.
"A bloke called Ten Bears, a Commanche leader, said that.

When the Chief told me about it, I thought it was so brilliant I asked him to write it down for me. I'm going to have it put on a tee shirt."

Dad started laughing.

"I was born where there were no enclosures... I want to die there and not within walls. What are you talking about man? You were born and bred on this estate, the wildest place you've ever been is Caerphilly town centre on a Saturday night."

Mr Harnett looked hurt. Mrs Harnett said, "We love the countryside. We go for a walk up to the camp with Buster every day. Must be a good mile, there and back."

She smiled at me.

"We've often seen your Kevin there."

Dad gave me a look.

"So you've joined bloody Tonto's fan club as well, have you? God is everyone around here but me completely crazy?"

Red Cloud and Pretty Hawk came out of Lo Cost, clutching carrier bags. I was sitting on the wall next to dad, Huw was in the jungle. We'd been there for ages, they were on their third can each.

Red Cloud saw me.

"Peace brother."

"Peace Red Cloud, peace Pretty Hawk."

"Christ!" said dad. He started laughing. I wished he wasn't there.

"This is my dad, that's his mate Huw, hiding behind the tree."

"Peace to you brothers. I am Red Cloud, this is my wife, Pretty Hawk."

"Alright love," said Dad, leering.

Huw giggled.

Pretty Hawk nodded. Her eyes were sad. She grabbed Red Cloud's arm.

"We must go. Come and visit us soon, Kevin."

Dad turned to me.

"You're spending too much time at that camp."

"So he should spend more time here, watching you drink?"

"I don't need any advice from you about how to bring up my kids, Hiawatha."

Red Cloud put down his carrier bags. He would have felled Dad with one blow if Pretty Hawk hadn't tugged his arm.

"Come on, let's go."

Dad and Red Cloud stared at each other for a few seconds. Then Red Cloud turned and left with Pretty Hawk. I wanted to go with them.

"Go on," said Dad, "Off you go. It's time to return your outfits to the fancy dress shop."

In the jungle Huw belched. He stepped away from the tree, stood next to dad.

"What do they look like, eh?"

"There you are! What the hell do you think you're playing at?"

It was the man from the open cast stall, pointing at Huw.

"You're sacked."

"No I'm not, I resign," said Huw, throwing back his head.

"There's people queueing up for these jobs. And don't think you can keep that costume either. I want it back — now!"

Afterwards, outside the shopping centre, Dad and Huw had another beer, and sang a rude song. When they'd finished, they stared into space.

"What are we going to do now?" said Huw.

It was the middle of the afternoon. Mam was still in her dressing gown, smoking a fag. She was talking on the phone to Aunt Janet, telling her about her new nightmare.

"I'm inside my own head, looking out, watching the water rising. The higher it gets, the more difficult it is to breathe. I'm watching the level slowly go up and up — above my mouth, then my nose. Every night I wake up gasping for breath just as the water's reaching my eyes. I know that as soon as it goes over my eyes, I'll die."

She paused, took a new fag from the packet, lit it with the end of the old one. Lyndon was swinging from the curtains, humming the Batman theme. Helen was ripping out pages from *Banzai You Bastards*!

"I'm frightened that one night I won't wake up in time."

"Dat! Dat!" shouted Helen, flinging dad's AC/DC cassettes across the room.

Mam wound the flex tighter and tighter round her finger.

"Him? Oh he's down the betting shop, blowing the last of his redundancy on another sure thing."

Suddenly Helen started crying; it sounded like somebody dragging a shard of glass across a concrete floor.

"It's all very well for you to say get out of there, but where am I supposed to go?"

The hand holding her fag started to shake.

"Stay with you till I sort myself out? Let me think about it."

"After what I saw at Aberfan," said Red Cloud.

Dad had asked him what had made him become an Indian. He'd had a big smirk on his face, but now his expression changed. He'd arrived at the camp with a bottle of whisky in one hand, a fag in the other.

"Come on Little Plum, you're coming home with me. It's late, your mam's worried."

It was getting dark. Before Dad arrived Red Cloud had offered to walk back to the reservation with me, but I didn't want to go. Dad sat down on the other side of the fire, unscrewed the cap from the bottle, took a swig, then held it out to Red Cloud. He shook his head.

"I have not touched a drop for thirty years."

"Bully for you."

Red Cloud took his time, finished rolling his cigarette, then lit it before he spoke again.

"There was a newsflash at 10.30 that morning. A slag heap had slid down the hill onto the primary school below in Aberfan. About twenty of us left work straight away and drove up there, it's only about twenty miles from Cardiff."

He tilted his head, as if hearing something in the distance, something too far away for me or dad to catch.

"Red Cloud will never forget the scene that greeted him. Smoke wafted up from the buried houses. A car was squashed under the tip, the horn blaring away. Further down, a whole terrace of houses had been flattened, a mountain of black waste filled the streets. There were hundreds of us clawing at the bricks and rubble. Every now and then a whistle blew, and everyone stopped. Lorry drivers switched off their engines, bulldozers came to a halt, there was complete silence. We held our breath, hoping for some sound that would let us know they'd found someone still alive. But it never happened. Instead they'd carry out a body draped in a blanket, the whistle would blow again, and we went back to work without a word."

Red Cloud took a long drag from his cigarette, leaned his head back, let the smoke stream through his nostrils. Wood crackled and shifted in the fire. Dad bent his head, ran his thumb around the neck of the bottle. Red Cloud flicked away some ash, carried on.

"I'd noticed that the blue ambulances from Merthyr always went to the hospital, while the others went to the mortuary. That made me think we were doing some good. It took me a while to realise that the blue ambulances weren't carrying survivors but people who'd worked themselves into a state of collapse."

He paused, staring at the glowing tip of the cigarette between his fingers. Above us in the fading light, swallows circled.

"I'll never forget one little girl they brought out from the rubble, still clutching an apple."

"Was she alive?" asked dad.

Red Cloud shook his head. The girl who had visited Red Cloud in his memory that day at the river.

"The firemen, the civil defence workers, the police, they knew it would take a miracle for us to find anyone alive, I saw it in their faces. But how could you stop? We worked through to the early hours of the morning, and that night we slept in a chapel. I remember thinking where was god when this happened? Had he been paying attention? Was he on his tea break?"

Dad laughed bitterly.

"The next day, Saturday, it began to rain in the afternoon. The tip was moving again, very slowly. More people kept coming, hundreds of them, standing around in the rain, watching. They turned my stomach. Then a man next to me collapsed from exhaustion and there was a scramble to grab his shovel and take his place. I realised they weren't sightseers, but simply waiting for the chance to help. That was the good part of Aberfan, the thing that I always tried to remember afterwards."

Red Cloud closed his eyes, took a long, deep breath before continuing.

"I returned to my white man's life. But I found that the things that had made me happy before — a few pints with my mates, going to football, chasing women — no longer brought any joy. I felt guilty all the time, why had I survived when all those children had died? I went to many different churches to try and find an answer. A Methodist told me that it wasn't fair to make God a scapegoat, that he'd given warnings, through the flooding and earlier slides. A Catholic pointed to the crucifix on the wall, saying 'That is what happened to god's only son, if He hadn't spared Jesus, why should we expect Him to interfere with other events?'"

Red Cloud shook his head.

"The only thing that would dull the pain was drink. Soon I couldn't even get through the morning without it, there was always a half bottle of vodka in my locker at work."

I couldn't imagine Red Cloud drinking so much. He always seemed so calm.

"Each day I needed to drink more to stop the pain. I thought I would never find peace. One drunken night, I decided to walk down to the docks and throw myself in. As I stood on the edge, looking down into the water I heard a voice say, 'This is not your real life. Your name is Red Cloud. Find the true way, then help others to do the same.' The Great Spirit had revealed himself to me."

I looked at dad, expecting him to make a joke, but he was staring at Red Cloud intently, no hint of a smile on his face.

"The white man is a parasite, always taking far more than he needs, never thinking of the future. His greed knows no bounds, he thinks only of himself. We are nothing to him. Do you think that they would have let such a terrible mountain of waste be built over Eton or Harrow?"

Dad shook his head, took another long swig of whisky.

"This land is all we have left. We cannot let them destroy it all over again. What will be left for our children?"

Dad didn't say anything till we reached the edge of the estate.

"My father went to Aberfan to help. I'd just started school

that year. When he came back, he walked across the room, grabbed me and held me so close I could hardly breathe. My mother had to tug him away from me, I started crying, I didn't realise what was happening."

He emptied the last of the whisky, chucked the bottle into the grass.

"He never talked about it. Even when he was drunk, which was most of the bloody time."

"So you had a chat with this Indian Chief, did you?" asked mam. "What was he like?"

Dad put down his fried egg sandwich, wiped his mouth. He missed a bit, there was still a bit of yolk on his chin.

"A nutter."

We stopped at the Job Centre on the way to the supermarket. Huw was just coming out.

"Anything new?" asked dad.

"Security guards," replied Huw. "They're recruiting loads. I reckon they must want them to help evict the protesters."

"Are you going to apply for it?"

Huw shook his head.

"How about you?"

Dad sighed, "I could do with the money."

I held my breath.

He clenched his jaw.

"No, I'm not working for those bloody parasites."

He looked embarrassed. He said goodbye to Huw, touched me on the shoulder.

"Come on Kevin, let's go."